133 Maths

PRESENTED
TO

Andrew Lane

from

Sam Hill

Sunday-School

1974 - 75

THE TIMPITTERS' MINE

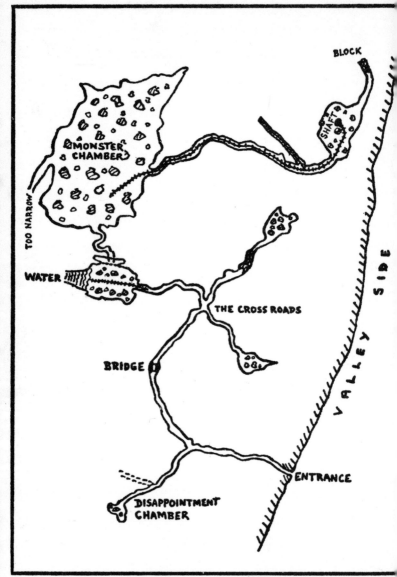

Dragon's Claw Mine

The Timpitters' Mine

by

CHRISTOPHER WRIGHT

VICTORY PRESS
LONDON and EASTBOURNE

Printed in Great Britain for
VICTORY PRESS (Evangelical Publishers Ltd.),
Lottbridge Drove, Eastbourne, Sussex,
by Compton Printing Ltd.,
London and Aylesbury

CONTENTS

Chapter 1

AN OLD PRINT

Peter Darlow and Tim Pryor stared at the old engraving hanging crookedly in the junk-shop.

"It is Hasslow; I'm sure it is!" exclaimed Peter with a certain amount of excitement.

"Yes," agreed Tim, dubiously.

"It is! Look how the village lies at the mouth of the valley. Let's ask how much it is."

"You can have it for three bob!"

Both boys jumped. They hadn't seen the old man standing in the shadows. Actually, Peter had noticed something but thought it was part of the general disarray of so-called antiques.

They fished in their pockets and managed to buy the print for half-a-crown—all they had.

"A bargain," announced Peter when they unwrapped it at Tim's house. They both knew Hasslow well, for they often stayed in that part of Derbyshire. They did so many things together that they had somehow become known as the Timpitters. Last year they had spent part of their summer holidays exploring the caves of the Peak District, staying at Hasslow Vicarage where Peter's uncle was vicar. Knowing the village so well explained their interest in the old print.

"Even allowing for the artist's imagination,"

said Tim, "things seem to have changed a bit. This road, or track, has disappeared now, and that building half-way up the hill which it leads to has gone. I wonder what it was; probably some old hermit's home."

"In which case he must have had a lot of visitors if it's got a track. I thought the whole point of being a hermit was to be lonely. I imagine this horse and cart has just been visiting him and—*Great Scott!*—it's got miners on board!"

"So what?" said Tim. "I imagine they were lead miners and not coal miners."

"That's what I'm Great Scotting about," said Peter excitedly. "Unless the old man held lead miners' tea parties, that black patch behind the building on the hill is a lead mine, *but it isn't there now*. That isn't a hermit's house. It's part of the missing mine of Hasslow—Dragon's Claw Mine. It was haunted or something, and the story goes that no one will ever be able to find it again. But we're going to prove the legend wrong," Peter cried, slapping Tim on the back. "We're going to dig it out this summer and explore it thoroughly. Just think of that: exploring a centuries-old lead mine for a holiday!"

They could both see the exciting possibilities of this discovery. Suddenly their troubles were over. Peter had been planning to go away with his parents, but shortly before the end of the summer term his grandmother had been taken ill and this meant that his parents had had to go away to look after her. He was now staying with his friend, Tim

Pryor, but both boys were unable to decide what to do with themselves when the holidays came.

Tim said he had never heard of this mysterious mine so Peter explained the little he knew. Although the village did not care to talk about the mine, it had apparently been used up to the middle of the last century when for some unaccountable reason it had suddenly been abandoned.

Outsiders assumed that the lead supply had run out, but the older villagers hinted that there were other reasons for its closure. But whether these reasons were real or imaginary, no one could tell. Indeed, why should they want to? The mine had disappeared and that was that—or was it?

Hasslow was built when lead mining in Derbyshire was at its peak, during the seventeenth century. Now that there was little money to be made from lead mining, most people farmed or catered for tourists. The church attracted some tourists and so did the river.

The river ran right down the valley and through the village. Some people fished in it and others complained that it made the village damp. In very wet weather there was certainly trouble from flooding, but for most of the year it was well-behaved.

Peter had built up such a liking for the village that it was hardly surprising that he should want to be back there again. It was here, too, that he had come to realise what it really meant to become a Christian. Probably because of his liking for Hasslow, he had a long dream that night in which he was back looking for the mine.

It was one of those silly, muddled sort of dreams, but Peter went straight to Tim's room the next morning to tell him about it. Peter was quite enthusiastic about the dream, but Tim could see no connection between emptying elephants out of dustbins and looking for the mine. Peter assured him it was all tied up in the dream.

"Anyway," said Peter, changing the subject rapidly, "I'll get my clothes and finish dressing in here. We'll have our Q.T. together, if you like."

Every morning and evening both Peter and Tim would have their own 'Quiet Time' when they would read a short bit from the Bible and talk to God. They called it 'Q.T.' for short.

Tim agreed and Peter returned with a heap of clothing in his arms. Soon they were both down at breakfast.

"Good gracious, you are early today!" exclaimed Mrs. Pryor. "Usually Tim has a last-minute scramble and now he's down before breakfast is even ready!"

Mrs. Pryor paused while the dog had a short barking session.

"He always barks at the new postman," she explained. "He hasn't got used to him yet."

Peter swung his fist against the door.

"I shouldn't do that," remarked Tim thoughtfully. "It isn't good for the paint!"

"I've just remembered," said Peter, smiling ruefully. "I haven't been home to see about *our* post yet, and I guess there's enough milk there to feed a cats' home!"

"There won't be," said Tim. "I saw a note saying 'No milk today, please', but we'd better see about your post on the way to school."

They just had time to make this call and Peter was surprised to find two letters for himself. There was no time for letter-reading just then, so he stuffed them in his pocket until he got to school. During break he read them properly.

The first was from his parents, enquiring after his welfare and giving him the latest news from their end. Would he be sure to let Mrs. Pryor have his dirty clothes for washing, and look in at Mrs. Freeman's to see his young brother, Michael, who was staying there? Other motherly advice and requests were included, but the inclusion of a ten shilling note was a very practical thought.

The second letter was an unexpected one from his uncle in Hasslow, who wrote:

Dear Peter,

Aunt Mary and myself are very sorry to hear about Granny's illness and we hope she will have a speedy recovery.

I imagine you have mixed feelings about being left without your parents, but I expect you will have great fun with Tim. I hear from your father than your planned family holiday in Devon has had to pass, so I expect you will be at rather a loose end. We should like to have you here again but I am going on holiday. I don't expect the new vicar who is taking my place would want two dirty boys running wild in the house.

I'm sure he wouldn't object to your sleeping in the coach-house loft, but I expect you already have other plans fixed. Should, however, you and Tim like to try it, don't hesitate to ask.

Aunt Mary wonders whether you have yet recovered from eating all those apples and I think it's a most unkind thought, although if I know anything about it you've already eaten the Pryors out of house and home!

Please remember me to Tim.

> Yours affectionately,
> Uncle Jack.

Peter smiled as he remembered the overeating incident. "Good old Uncle," he thought. "Still as good as ever. Great idea, sleeping in the coach-house. I'll tell Tim about it on the way home."

Tim was very enthusiastic about the idea but asked, "What do you think your parents will say about this?"

Peter took on one of his occasional serious airs. "I've thought about that, and I'm writing to Mother and Father today. I think Dad will say it's okay. I know he's interested in Dragon's Claw Mine because I heard him discussing it with Uncle Jack once. Come to that, I could write to Uncle Jack and ask him if he can tell us anything about it. Anyway, I don't think we need bother about that. After all, we've been caving together before. The main problem is going to be getting the equipment we'll need for exploring. I wonder if the school Caving Club would help us there."

"Well, write and tell your parents what we hope to do, and *then* we'll see what else there is to be done." Tim was being cautious. Then he added, "And don't forget, if we do go, I want to re-visit that interesting cave at Eyam!"

Chapter 2

RIVALS

That afternoon the two boys were to be found busy in the City Reference Library, reading old books for references of Dragon's Claw Mine, without much success. In despair Peter had taken his problem to one of the librarians who had been most helpful.

"I believe there was a book published in the early nineteenth century dealing with lead mining in Derbyshire, but I'm not sure who wrote it," she said quietly, being mindful of the other people reading. "But we can soon find out in our files."

They waited while the librarian plunged into dusty depths, and their hopes rose when they saw her returning with an old, battered book.

"I think this is the book you want," she said breathlessly. "It deals with mines and agriculture, which seem rather a funny mixture, but be careful with it because I believe it's rather valuable."

"Pretty dusty, isn't it?" whispered Tim as they tiptoed to an empty table.

"Yes, you can almost hear the spiders knocking to be let out!"

With this comment from Peter, Tim exploded as one does when taken by a joke unawares, and the two suddenly became conscious of eyes looking

14

at them over the tops of tables, from all directions.

"We'd better sit down and shut up," said Peter dryly. "We've caused enough disturbance already. I don't particularly want to get thrown out."

They settled down together and thumbed through the index. To their disappointment there was no reference to Dragon's Claw Mine, but there was plenty of information about mining in general which they read with interest. The problem was once more brought to the librarian, who told them that she could help them no further with books.

"I think the best thing you can do," she said, "is to write to one of the large Derbyshire mining companies to see if they can help you. They must have records of mines. You'll find a Derbyshire address list on the shelf marked 'Directories' over there."

The boys thanked her and were soon searching for addresses.

"This seems about the only one. H. Burgess & Co.," said Peter, pointing to a company in that district. "We'd better copy that down and get writing to them. It's really a quarry company but it's classified under mines."

On the way out they thanked the librarian for helping them.

"Jolly good of her," Peter said. "They're not always so helpful." Peter had had experience of what he called the 'unhelpful, older generation'.

"That book she got us was good," said Tim.

"Yes. Pity there was nothing about Dragon's Claw Mine, but that bit about how mines were made was good. I never thought there was so much to it. I imagined all you did was to dig tunnels and shafts. No wonder old mines aren't very safe where they are, or maybe were, supported by timber. I didn't realise that the floor and roof were often false, just resting on wooden boards. I guess all the wood rotted quickly and the miners couldn't use the mines for long."

"Does that mean Dragon's Claw Mine will have fallen in or be unsafe?" asked Tim, rather worried by this new outlook on things.

"Well, obviously the entrance has fallen in or been hidden, but that doesn't mean the whole lot's unsafe. The limestone in that area is pretty solid, so it might have been okay to build up bad parts with stone. We'll have to be careful but we should be able to tell what it's like once we're in."

Tim smiled at Peter's optimistic 'once we're in'.

"Fancy all those shafts not being entrances," Peter continued, "but only for ventilation and hauling stuff up. They must have fallen in often, though; so they wouldn't be very safe now, would they? Anyway, let's get home now and write that letter."

With this, Peter and Tim unlocked their cycles from the library railings and went back to the Pryors' house.

"I can't think what those Timpitters are up to now," said Mrs. Pryor as the two boys dashed upstairs as soon as tea was finished.

"I shouldn't worry about them," Mr. Pryor replied. "They're probably up to no good but at least they're quiet and out of the way."

A crash from upstairs shook the house.

"Well, at least they're out of the way."

In Tim's room the boys were endeavouring to write the letter to the quarry company but were having some difficulty.

"We'd better not let them know we're boys or they may not be so helpful," advised Tim, speaking from bitter experience. "It's funny, but some people think that young people exist only to waste time."

"Right," said Peter, taking out his pen and stretching his arm. "Let's get cracking on the draft. I suppose we'd better address it to the manager." He wrote:

Dear Sir,
    I am trying to get information about Dragon's Claw Mine, Hasslow, but so far have been unable to do so. It has been suggested that you might have some records about it which you could lend me. Failing this, could you suggest anywhere I might get some information?

"There!" said Peter. "How's that for a professional job? All we need now is some decent paper and we'll do it properly."

They decided that Tim should copy the letter as Peter's writing was so hard to read.

"I'll write to Uncle Jack," said Peter, once Tim was started on the job. "He may be able to help. There might still be in existence some old parish records that mention it. There's no harm in trying, and, in any case, I must thank him for offering us the coach-house loft."

Tim was ending the letter to the quarry and finished with a magnificent signature.

"I say!" exclaimed Peter when he saw it. "How did you manage that? Whenever I try one it looks so awful that I have to re-write the whole letter."

"Oh, it just comes naturally," Tim explained, and then laughed as he continued: "Actually it was most unexpected. I've never done it before and I don't expect I'll ever do it again."

"Perhaps you'd better cut it out and frame it," suggested Peter. Then, pretending to be annoyed, he went on: "I wish you'd shut up, or I'll be writing the most dreadful drivel to Uncle."

They hoped for replies to their letters by Tuesday, but that day seemed a long time coming. When it did at last arrive there were two letters to reward their impatience.

"This one's Uncle Jack's," said Peter, looking at the writing and postmark. He tore it open, skimmed through it and then started reading it aloud for Tim's benefit.

Dear Peter,

Thank you for your letter enquiring for details about Dragon's Claw Mine. I can't think where you got your information giving a clue to its whereabouts but I shan't probe into your secrets.

I am writing by return post as I know you will be impatient for a reply, and I am entirely in sympathy with you. I shall write to the vicar who is taking my place this summer, letting him know you want to sleep in the coach-house loft. Naturally you will have to provide your own meals etc., but Aunt Mary will leave some blankets and things out for you which you can collect from the house. The name of the vicar is the Rev. John Parkinson whose parish is in the Midlands.

I am afraid that there are no records of the mine in the parish but I am enclosing a cutting from the local paper which was published about thirty years ago, when a fairly thorough search was made for it. The 'old man on the moor' who is mentioned must be Mad Sam. He seems to know some sort of secret about the mine but I think he is best left alone. You may remember him.

The search was made when there was a rumour of the mine being still workable—not only for lead but for fluorspar which is used in the manufacture of steel. As you can see on reading it, the searchers didn't meet with much success.

However, I wish you two mine hunters all the best.

Yours affectionately,
Uncle Jack.

"Well," demanded Tim, "where's the cutting?"

"Perhaps Uncle Jack forgot to put it in. Oh no, here it is," said Peter, peering into the envelope.

The two boys spread it on the table and started to read. It began with a rather gripping headline.

MISSING MINE PUZZLES EXPERTS

Mine and quarry experts have been searching unsuccessfully during the past week for Dragon's Claw Mine in the valley of Hasslow, and they have now abandoned all hope of finding it.

Now that the value of fluorspar has increased, the re-opening of it might have proved profitable, with the possible discovery of new minerals. Throughout the search, however, the mine eluded its searchers.

One or two things have puzzled the experts. Firstly, although mine records must have been kept, they all appear to have been destroyed. Secondly, the older villagers have declined to talk about the matter and were almost hostile. Thirdly, one old man living all alone on the bleak moors kept dropping hints to the searchers of hauntings, danger and the mine never being found. Evidently his grandfather had mined there.

Opened in the sixteenth century, Dragon's Claw Mine had a rich lead source which made a profitable livelihood for the village, but since its disappearance, or closure, mineral working in the village has ceased altogether. Some of the villagers now work in nearby quarries. The mine was believed to have nearly half a mile of workings, together with many natural parts.

Amongst these natural parts there is supposed to be a very large chamber. It is because of things like this that interest in the mine has been aroused.

The quarry company of Messrs. Burgess & Sons, who were in charge of the operations, have now moved to nearby Little Wilton where ground will be surveyed for fresh mineral supplies . . .

The report then continued with a description of the methods used in mineral surveying and general information on their use in industry.

"That's pretty good," said Peter, after they had read it through twice. "Not only is the mine lost, but there really *does* seem to be a mystery about it. I can just picture the report in the same paper when *we* find the place. 'Two School Boys Succeed Where Experts Fail', or something like that."

"How about 'Two School Boys Find Missing Mystery Mine'?" suggested Tim. "Anyway, let's open the second letter which we seem to have forgotten about."

Peter opened it and announced: "It's from the quarry company. By the way, did you notice it's the same one that was looking for the mine thirty years ago? They say that they have no record of the mine but they did search for it some years ago. That must have been the search the cutting was written about."

Peter paused for breath and then continued: "Although they made a search, they have no information of value that would help us and . . . Oh my!"

He groaned and pulled a face, letting the letter fall on the table. Tim picked it up and started reading to see what Peter had exclaimed about.

"Although," he read, "the previous search was unsuccessful, we have planned another search this summer, using modern methods which no doubt will be completely successful."

"No doubt they will," said Peter dryly. "But that doesn't help us at all."

"Never mind; we'll be able to go after they've found it." Tim was trying to be optimistic.

"Don't be daft!" said Peter. "They won't let us in if it's being worked. In any case, we want to find it *ourselves*, not stand by and let someone else find it."

"In that case," said Tim, "we'll have to go as soon as term ends and hope we find it before they do. We might even sell it to them!"

Peter was brightening up and laughed at this suggestion of Tim's. "I should doubt it very much as it isn't our land. The quarry company will have to get permission from the land-owner before they can just dig away. Come to that, so will we."

"Supposing we can't?" Tim was troubled at the idea. "Anyway. whose land is it?"

"I don't know. Get our two-and-a-half inch map and we'll have a look. We were daft not to plot it onto the map before."

At this stage, Mr. Pryor walked into the room. "I don't know if the two of you are intending to go to school today but, just in case you are, I thought I'd better let you know you'll be late."

"*School?* Oh no!" cried the two together, and they fled from the house in a great flurry.

Mr. Pryor stood at the door and watched them go. As they disappeared from view he smiled to himself and went into the house.

"You know, dear," he said to his wife, "even *I* am starting to get intrigued by the behaviour of those boys. They rush about enough as it is *now*; I shudder to think what will happen when they break up on Friday. We'll have to reinforce the staircase!"

For Peter at school, the day dragged on and on as though it would never end. The masters were being more lenient now and allowing the boys to amuse themselves. This only seemed to make the day go more slowly.

Tim was in a different form from Peter, so they could see each other only during break. At last the bell rang the happy news that school was over for another day, and two hopeful explorers made their way home to be met with a piece of devastating news. Mrs. Pryor was at the door to meet them. As the boys wheeled their cycles up the path, Tim said to Peter:

"Something's up; I can see by the way Mum's smiling."

"Mrs. Freeman has kindly offered to have both of you to tea today."

Tim's younger brother and sister were leering in the background.

"You haven't accepted, have you?" asked Tim with a note of panic in his voice. "We're busy to-night."

"I had to, Tim. Once you're there I expect you'll enjoy it. At first she asked just Peter as it's his brother staying with her, but when I said you were here, too, she asked you as well. I thought you'd rather go together."

"That's all right," consoled Peter. "We do owe it to her. She must be having a rotten job looking after Michael! Although, why she should want us as well, I can't imagine! We'll be home later this evening and we can do all we want to then. I'm glad Tim's coming, though." He winked at Tim.

"Well, run in and get washed now," said Mrs. Pryor, pleased at the way Peter had handled the situation. "You'll have to be leaving in a minute, so look sharp."

Chapter 3

HINTS OF UNREST

It was not too late when they returned from Mrs. Freeman's, and both boys had enjoyed themselves as Tim's mother had anticipated. Once they had put their cycles away, it did not take them long to get upstairs and find the two-and-a-half inch map of the Hasslow area.

Plotting where the mine could be was more difficult than they had expected, as there was no definite landmark to fix it with. According to the print, the mine was half-way down one side of a steep valley, shown on the map as three hundred and fifty feet deep. On the opposite side of the valley to the mine, a smaller valley ran away. Behind the mine there was open moorland of the type so frequently found in the Peak District. All around, especially on the moorland, numerous 'Old Lead Mines' were marked, and this explained a problem to the boys.

"No wonder the mine is so hard to find," said Peter. "With all these old shafts and workings about, you'd never know where to begin. All the same, it won't be so hard with the modern scientific methods . . . Hang on; your mother's calling."

They opened the bedroom door and went to the banisters.

"Peter," Mrs. Pryor called, "your mother is on the phone for you."

"My parents? I guess they've phoned to say if I can go caving or not," he told Tim as they dashed downstairs. "They'll have got my letter this morning." Then over the phone: "Hello . . . Yes, Mum . . . Fine, thanks . . . Yes . . ."

Tim stood by, waiting and wondering.

"Yes . . . Oh, nothing much. What about? . . . Yes . . . *I can! Oh, fine!*" Peter smiled at Tim and nodded violently. "We want to go as soon as term ends . . . Yes, it finishes Friday . . . Oh, Uncle's written to you, has he . . . ?"

Tim took no further interest in the conversation and went smiling into the sitting-room to wait until Peter had finished.

Mr. Pryor put down the evening paper and looked hard at Tim, who laughed.

"Well, well, you are happy tonight, Tim. Are you going to let me into your secret? I'm very intrigued you know."

"I might as well tell you." Tim lay back in an armchair and started at the beginning, from the finding of the print. Just as he finished, Peter came into the room.

"I've just been telling Dad our plans," Tim explained. Then he turned to his father and asked, "Do you think we can go? Do say yes."

"I have no objections, but I don't know what Peter's parents will have to say about it."

"If they say yes," said Tim cunningly, "can we go?"

"If they say yes, then I'll talk the matter over with your mother, Tim." Mr. Pryor was being cautious.

"They have done! They have done!" Tim had left his chair and was almost dancing on the floor.

At that moment the door opened and Mrs. Pryor walked in.

"Good gracious!" she exclaimed. "Whatever is all the noise about?"

"You two run along now," said Mr. Pryor, "and I'll explain everything."

"Do your best, won't you, Dad?" was Tim's parting remark as he and Peter closed the door, leaving a very puzzled mother behind.

"I hope everything's okay, Peter," said Tim as they ascended the stairs. "It would be awful for everything to be stopped at the last moment. Just when we've managed to scrounge some ladder and rope from the school Caving Club it's just . . ."

"Don't worry," interrupted Peter. "Your mother won't mind now my parents have given their consent. You see."

"Is it all right to pray about this sort of thing?" asked Tim.

"Good gracious, yes. This is just the sort of thing to share with Jesus. Then, if He has planned something different for you, it seems okay, somehow."

All the same, in spite of Peter's cheerfulness, their stomachs turned when they were called downstairs. But they were soon put at rest, and they sighed with relief at the good news. Plans had to be talked over, and it was quite late that night

when Peter and Tim, tired but excited, went upstairs to bed.

"Roll on Friday and end of term," yawned Tim.

"Better still Monday, when we leave."

"Nonsense, Peter, it will be great fun getting
ready. Anyway, we'd better be getting to bed."

"I suppose you're right," said Peter, now yawn-
ing himself. "Good-night."

A rather sleepy Q.T. and Peter climbed into
bed.

*   *   *

Friday afternoon came at last, and Peter and
Tim were sorting out all their kit on the floor in
Tim's room. Peter was fingering the thin, wire
ladders and nylon ropes lovingly.

In spite of the boys' fear of forgetting things, a
heap of terrifying size rose on the floor, and by
the time the boys were ready for bed the heap was
even larger.

That night Tim was soon asleep but Peter lay
on his bed and thought. The night was rather
warm and he found he could not sleep even when
he tried. So he resigned himself to this and lay
planning. He pictured caves, mines, underground
waterfalls and caverns until he finally dropped off
to sleep.

Waking early the next morning he felt too lazy
to get up, so he reached out a sleepy hand and
picked up the large scale map of the Hasslow area
that was lying on the table by the side of his bed.

He stared at it vacantly for a moment or two until his mind and eyes focussed on the print; then he found the vicarage. After looking at that for a minute, he found the side of the valley where they supposed the mine to be.

Before he could do much, Tim came staggering sleepily into the room.

"I've only just woken up," he explained, flopping down on the side of Peter's bed. "I thought I'd better get you up; there's still plenty to do."

"Nonsense!" retorted Peter as he hastily retreated under the bedclothes.

"Have you tried to see how far the mine goes in if we assume that there are half a mile of workings?" asked Tim, ignoring his friend's laziness.

"It's impossible to say, really," replied Peter, transferring the tips of his finger and thumb from the scale to the map. "But even if the passage is straight, and I don't suppose it is, it doesn't go anywhere special."

Tim leaned over and looked as Peter drew an imaginary arc from the supposed entrance.

"As you can see, Tim, nothing special is included. Oh yes, there's a building of some sort. See it? That's all. Probably an old lead mining shed. There are one or two around, but of course they're only ruins."

"I expect it's Mad Sam's house," said Tim, laughing. "But get up, do. We'll have our Q.T. together again, if you like. I don't imagine you've had yours yet!"

Peter came back to reality with a jolt, and with

C

an effort he climbed out of bed, assisted by a heart-
less Tim.

*   *   *

Monday seemed a long time coming, and the
train journey seemed even longer.

Getting out at Hasslow Station, they were recognised by the station master who greeted them in
his broad Derbyshire accent.

"Hello," he said. "Have you come to stay
again?"

"Yes," said Peter, while he and Tim shook
hands.

"Well," the station master continued, "I suppose you've just come in time for the excitement."

"Really?" Peter exclaimed. "What excitement
is this?"

The station master thought for a moment and
then pointed towards Hasslow Moor. "See yon
moor?" he said. "Well, for past week there's been
a mining company looking for the . . . er, a lost
mine."

"Have they found it yet?" asked Tim anxiously.

"Nay, lad, and I don't reckon they will."

"Why not?" Tim was curious but tried not to
sound too interested.

"Well, you see . . ." The station master stopped
and cleared his throat. "I think you'd better be getting along now; I've work to do," he said rather
sharply, as though he had said more than he meant.

"Oh tell us, do," pleaded Peter.

"It's nothing. Just something I thought of. Now look, there's Tom with a tractor and trailer; he'll take you to the village."

Tom was hailed and the two boys loaded their luggage on the trailer and waved good-bye to the station master.

"I hear you've got visitors on the moor, Tom," shouted Peter above the noise of the moving tractor.

"Aye, lad."

"The station master said they were looking for a mine but they'd never find it. Why did he say that?"

Tom either did not hear or pretended not to hear, so Peter repeated his question.

"Look, lad," burst out Tom, "whatever that company's doing is no business of ours, and we keep our noses out of what doesn't concern us."

"Well!" exclaimed Peter to Tim, who was sitting beside him on the trailer. "They don't exactly encourage us to talk about it, do they? I think that last remark of Tom's was directed against *us*."

The three remained in silence for the rest of the journey; but when they arrived at the vicarage, Tom, as though to make up for his behaviour on the journey, was most pleasant, but he made no mention of the mine. At the gates the two boys stopped to recover from the jolting of the trailer.

"Tom got quite shirty, didn't he?" said Peter, rather hurt by their friend's behaviour.

"I don't think he meant it, though, Peter. He must have felt a bit sore, but he didn't mean *us* any harm. I think his feelings were against the quarry company."

Still discussing the matter, they struggled up to the vicarage and rang the bell. The door was opened by the new vicar, the Reverend John Parkinson.

"Hello, boys," he said. "Come in for a bit and rest your weary limbs."

Gratefully, Peter and Tim went into the house which was nice and cool. Being old, it had thick walls that kept the heat out. Iced lemonade was gratefully accepted, and while drinking it they chatted to the vicar and his wife.

"The bedding and things are in the hall," said Mrs. Parkinson. "But I wonder if you'd be dears and pop down to the village before you settle in, to get me a couple of things. Would you mind?"

"Of course not," said Peter, getting to his feet. "I want to go down, anyway, and drop a letter in the post that I wrote in the train to Mum and Dad, telling them I'd arrived safely."

"You're very optimistic, Peter," said Mr. Parkinson, laughing.

"Well," explained Peter, laughing also, "I thought they'd worry less if they heard tomorrow. In any case, I *have* arrived, haven't I?"

Down in the village the atmosphere seemed restless. Of course, it might have been the boys' imagination, but outside the inn a few old men sat on benches with their heads bent together as though they were holding a secret meeting. The boys went into the shop and waited their turn. Mrs. Warner, who had owned the shop for years, did not seem as cheerful as she had in the past. When she served the boys she looked around as though there might be spies lurking in every corner, although there was no other customer in the shop at the time. Having thus satisfied herself that no one else was listening, she leaned over the counter and said quietly:

"Now don't go looking into the affairs of others."

Having given this strange piece of advice, she seemed rather embarrassed and disappeared into the back of the shop, leaving the two boys looking at each other.

Outside, the old men were huddled together by the inn, and as Peter and Tim passed them a lorry came rattling by. Heads rose to look at it and a murmur broke from them like a hive of angry bees. One man shouted something angrily after it, and there was a murmur of approval.

Tim looked at the tail-board of the lorry as it rounded the bend, and he noticed the name on the back. 'H. Burgess & Co. Mine and Quarry Works.' Peter also noticed it.

"Well, well," he said. "With every moment of the day, the mystery deepens."

Chapter 4

SETTLING IN

It was quite late the first morning when they awoke in their new surroundings. The sun was streaming through the coach house window, but in spite of this the loft was quite cold.

"I say!" Peter exclaimed. "I never thought it would be like this in the morning. I imagined a beautifully warm room. I expect it will soon warm up, though. Come on; let's get some breakfast going. I feel famished."

Soon the smell of frying and paraffin fumes was filling the coach house, making Peter's and Tim's mouths water. Both stoves were going and making quite a noise.

"Tim," said Peter above the roar, "does this bring back camping memories?"

"I'll say it does. It's one of the best smells in the world, I think; but don't sit there in a trance; the bacon's burning!"

The two boys ate their meal quickly as they were anxious to be off exploring. Plans for the day were once again discussed.

"I think it would be best to leave all our equipment here and just see the lie of the land," said Peter. "I shouldn't imagine we'll be able to explore the mine today. It will probably need digging out

34

and there may be tons of rock to move. I reckon the best thing to do is to try to find exactly where the mine is and then go and speak to the land owner, who, by the way, we haven't yet discovered. He might be able to lend us some tools to dig it out, unless he's also one of these strange types who won't talk about the place. Anyway, I expect it will take us most of our time to get it dug out."

"In which case, Peter, we might as well have the day out, although it's not very far to Hasslow Dale. We'll take sandwiches or something."

As Peter was putting the breakfast things away he heard footsteps crunching across the gravel. The two boys went to the window to see who their visitor was. Down below, Mr. Parkinson was standing, looking up at them.

"Did you have a good night?" he called up.

"Yes, thanks," answered Peter.

"Good. I say, something smells good. Mind if I come up?"

"No, do," called back Peter.

There was a scrabble on the loft steps and the trap-door swung open.

"Mmm, delicious. You've been breakfasting rather late, haven't you?"

Tim laughed. "Yes, we overslept rather, but it doesn't matter as we're spending the day out in Hasslow Dale."

Peter and Tim explained briefly the reason for their visit, and the vicar was extremely interested, but he tactfully refrained from offering any advice unless asked for it.

"Well," he said at last, half in and half out of the loft, "I mustn't stay, but drop in and see us when you return. We'd like to hear the latest report on your search, so have some tea with us. If you can time your return for about five o'clock, that would be fine."

"Thanks very much, said Peter, glad of the prospect of a prepared tea at the end of the day.

Wishing them good hunting, the vicar disappeared.

"That's jolly decent of him." Peter had taken an immediate liking to the vicar. "It's funny, you know, but some people have the weirdest ideas about clergymen. They think of them as anything but human. More like school teachers, in fact! Anyway, if you're ready, let's get going. I can't wait to get to Hasslow Dale."

"I *think* we've got everything," said Tim, having a last look round. "Oh, wait a moment; we've forgotten the camera."

At last they were ready and the two set off, armed with map, print, camera and sandwiches.

"Which way are we going?" asked Tim, as they paused at the vicarage gates.

"Let's cut up over the moor and get to the valley that way," suggested Peter. "Then we can see the quarry company at work. It should be rather interesting."

They agreed to do this and quickly took the road to the moor. The sun was chasing the early morning clouds out of the sky and there was a pleasant breeze blowing in their faces. Although the weather was unsettled, everything seemed in favour of a good day's outing.

They had been climbing steadily for some time when they paused to get their breath back.

"See that clump of bushes?" said Peter. "There's a small mine passage there. It doesn't go in very far, although there's a small shaft at the far end. It's only a few feet deep and that's the lot. I've often been in there before and know there's not much to it. You don't want to bother with it, do you?"

Tim didn't, so they continued to climb until at long last they reached the top.

"There's the valley over there," said Peter, pointing.

The wind was quite strong on top and they had to speak loudly to make themselves heard.

Peter continued, "I haven't been over this way much before, because it isn't the shortest route to the valley. This ground is pretty new to me from now on. It's jolly desolate, isn't it?"

"Yes. I can't see any sign of the quarry company, can you?"

"No—though wait a moment." Peter paused and listened.

On the wind, the sound of a lorry struggling in low gear could be heard. Both boys listened to it for a moment.

"I should think it's their lorry," said Peter, "although I can't see where the sound's coming from. It might be some distance away, though. See that small building right over there? That must be the small building marked on the map. Pity we haven't got any field glasses with us, or we could see if it's derelict or not. I'll get the map out and then we can see exactly where we are and find the best way across the moor. I don't feel like doing too much climbing now."

Once they had looked at the map, Peter was in favour of sitting down for a bit, but Tim was impatient to get going. So with a swig from the water bottle they moved on again. The moor was anything but smooth on top. All around were mysterious pits and piles of earth and stone.

"I believe they call it gruffy land," Peter explained.

"Why is it like this? I don't imagine it's natural."

"Oh, no. It's where minerals, probably lead in this case, have been worked on the surface. Then, as the book we read in the library said, if the vein of lead was good, the miners would follow it down and make a shaft. I expect that's one down there."

The boys were on the edge of the moor and about thirty yards below them was a pile of branches covering a hole in the ground, surrounded by a small barbed wire fence. Tim went galloping down the slope towards it.

"Hey, watch it!" called Peter, who was following carefully behind. "Don't go too fast or you may not be able to stop in time. It may be jolly deep."

Tim waited for Peter to catch him up, and they both approached with care.

"Don't go inside the barbed wire," cautioned Peter. "The sides of the shaft are only earth and they could easily crumble away if we stood there, apart from the danger of overbalancing."

Peter picked up a large stone and heaved it in. There was a crash as it hit the brush-wood and tore through. Then a moment of silence was followed by a deep crash as the stone smashed to smithereens far below. Tim found an even larger stone that could only be rolled in. This hit the side of the shaft almost at once and took some time booming and bouncing its way to the bottom. Even after the final crash, the sound of falling stone continued, as bits dislodged by the large stone clattered downwards.

The boys stood back at a respectful distance.

"Phew!" exclaimed Tim, wiping his hands on his trousers. "How deep do you reckon it is?"

"I don't know," said Peter, "but we can work it out. We'll throw another stone in and then count how long it takes. As long as it doesn't hit the sides it should be okay. If it hits, of course, it will slow it down a lot."

They threw another stone and Peter counted three slowly before the stone hit the bottom. He did a quick calculation and then said excitedly:

"It's about two hundred feet. That's jolly deep, you know."

Tim wanted to throw another stone to hear the booming sound it made, but Peter advised him not to, as it might dislodge the branches covering the hole, which were already very few. Just as they turned to go, Tim pulled out his handkerchief to blow his nose and a sixpence dropped down. He made a grab at it but it rolled down the slope and disappeared over the edge of the shaft. As it tinkled its way to the bottom, Tim stood by looking grief stricken.

"Don't worry too much," laughed Peter, amused by his friend's expression. "You've hardly lost a fortune."

With these deeply comforting words of Peter's, Tim mumbled something about sixpences not growing on trees and then grinned. With a struggle they made their way back to the top of the moor.

Chapter 5

THUNDER AND A MEETING

The weather was certainly unsettled. Although the sun was out the wind made it feel quite cold. The clouds looked thundery. The boys started to run. The wind was against them and their hair was being blown all over the place. They had been jogging along for some time when Peter suddenly stopped.

"What's the matter?" asked Tim, realising that Peter had stopped rather suddenly if it was just to get his breath back.

"There's the lorry we saw yesterday," said Peter, absently staring in front of him.

They had come to a part of the moor where the ground suddenly dropped at a natural slope which had been dug into, making an earthy cliff. Down below was a lorry and a group of men.

"Don't make any noise," said Peter, coming back to life again. "We'll spy on them for a bit and then go down."

Quietly they lay down on the edge and, with their faces half hidden by heather, watched the men at work. They appeared to have just finished a tea-break, for they were picking up tools and instruments. The wind was making too much noise for them to hear much of what was being said, and they could catch only occasional words. There were four workmen in overalls and two men in tweed caps and sports coats, who were obviously the surveyors.

Sticking in the ground at intervals were poles coloured with red, white and black bands. The two surveyors walked over to one of these and measured out a distance with a tape.

"They've got quite a set-up, haven't they, Tim?" said Peter. "This must be their permanent base, judging by the stuff they have here."

He was referring to the two huts and temporary road cleared of grass and heather. They watched for some time until they felt cold again. Dark clouds had been creeping over the sky, that they had not noticed.

"I should think we're in for rain before long," said Peter, "so let's go down."

They slithered down the slope in a shower of earth and stones. The surveyors had gone over a rise and were not in sight, but the workmen were digging a hole and were obviously startled by this sudden intrusion. They all looked up from their work and one of them shouted something.

"What did he say?" asked Tim.

"I don't know, but it doesn't sound as though we're being welcomed with open arms!"

The shouting was renewed.

"Perhaps they're cannibals," suggested Peter, "so it might be wise to withdraw."

Before they could do anything, however, the men approached threateningly with their picks and spades.

"Go on, clear orf, will yer!" they shouted.

"We only came to see what was happening," said Peter, retreating, not sure what was going to happen next but having horrible suspicions.

"Came to see what was happening, did yer? If you don't clear orf, something will be happening."

"We didn't mean any harm." Peter realised it was useless trying to explain.

At that moment one of the surveyors appeared on the scene.

"Now, then, what's the matter?" he asked.

"We found them poking their noses into things," said one of the men, who had gone purple in the face through shouting.

"Well," said the surveyor, "there's no need to bite their heads off." He turned to the boys. "Are you interested in mining? Because if you are, come inside and I'll show you what we're doing."

He motioned the boys towards a hut. "I'm sorry about the behaviour of my workmen," he said, "but things are a bit strained all round at the moment."

"I think," said Peter, laughing, "that you arrived just in time to prevent bloodshed. But still, it was quite exciting while it lasted. I'm Peter and this is Tim. We call ourselves the Timpitters, for fairly obvious reasons."

The surveyor peered at Peter. "That badge," he said, pointing at Peter's pullover. "My boy wears one of those. Isn't it a Bible class or something?"

Peter nodded, and Tim showed that he wore one, too.

The surveyor looked puzzled. "Well, you look pretty normal!" He laughed, while Peter and Tim stood amazed. "I didn't mean any disrespect. I've never had much time for religion," he explained. "When my boy joined this group I thought it might be a lot of cranks. Obviously I was wrong, although my boy has started reading his Bible."

"So do we," said Tim, taking a deep breath.

"You *what*? Oh well, I suppose it's one of those things you grow out of," he said kindly, obviously trying to understand the boys.

Tim decided to take the plunge. "You don't grow out of that sort of thing unless it never meant anything to you. I started a few months ago when I became a Christian. I must admit I never bothered before then," he confessed with a grin.

The surveyor still looked puzzled. "I don't follow you," he said. "People don't *become* Christians —unless," he added as an after-thought, "unless they have some foreign religion."

"What do you think a Christian is, then?" asked Peter.

"Well, someone who goes about doing the right things, I suppose."

"Don't a lot of people who have a foreign religion do this?" asked Peter.

The surveyor looked even more puzzled. "Yes, they do. I suppose all religions are much the same, in that case. Does it matter which one you follow?"

It was Tim's turn to reply. "Other religions say that people get to heaven by being good. The Bible says that because we are sinful in God's sight we can never get to heaven that way."

Somehow it was possible to say these things to someone who was interested and not making fun of them. Tim continued:

"I know *I'm* going to heaven because Jesus has said that if I ask Him to forgive my sins and to take charge of my life He will make me one of His children."

Tim paused for a moment to recover. Fancy being able to say this, and in the middle of Hasslow Moor!

"Do you *really* believe that?" asked the surveyor.

"Not only do I believe it, but over the last few months I've found it to be true."

"You know, you've both set me thinking. It seems as though my boy's onto something after all."

A shout came from outside.

"Excuse me a minute; I'm wanted."

He was gone only a short while, but when he came back he had obviously thought it was time for a change of subject. "Tell me why you've come," he invited.

There was an awkward silence and then Tim said, "Perhaps you can clear up a mystery for us. We find that the villagers of Hasslow don't like your working here. Why?"

At the mention of Hasslow, the surveyor winced but seemed relieved that the matter had been brought up.

"I'll tell you," he said. "You may, or may not, know that we are looking for a lost mine."

Peter nodded but did not interrupt.

"Now we want to find this mine as it may be of value to us. The villagers of Hasslow appear to have some absurd legend about the mine which says that working it will spell death to the village. It's quite foolish but we can't convince them that it is. Of course, this mine is not the only thing we're looking for. There are probably other mineral deposits around here but so far we have drawn blanks all round. There's also a legend that the mine will never be found, but they don't appear to have much faith in that one, judging by the way they're dead set against us! There is, in fact, almost a state of war."

He then told them how they searched for minerals.

"And what," asked Peter casually, when the surveyor had finished, "do you think your chances are of finding this lost mine?"

The surveyor thought for a few moments and then said, "There's more to this than there first appears to be. The entrance must have been blocked up so we will have to dig a new way in. The trouble is that there are so many mine workings in this area that we might spend a fortune digging into a mine hardly big enough to turn round in. We must be sure that we've located the right mine before we dig. Anyway, I must get back to work now, but it's been nice seeing you. Thanks for calling. Are you from the village?"

"We're staying at the vicarage," explained Peter. "I know this area well, though, as I often come to stay here."

"Fine. Drop in next time you're passing, won't you? You can have the latest report on our progress. My name is Wheeler. Oh, and I'll have a word with the workmen so you don't get massacred. You wouldn't like to stay for a bit now and watch us working, would you?"

"We'd like to," said Peter, "but we ought to be getting on; the sky looks heavy. Perhaps next time. Thanks a lot, Mr. Wheeler. Cheerio." Then to Tim, "Come on; race you to that hawthorn."

Both boys charged up the slope, leaving four very puzzled workmen behind, shaking their heads and muttering. The boys reached the tree and stood panting.

"Well," gasped Tim, "things seemed to brighten up a bit after that brilliant welcome they gave us. Mr. Wheeler was okay. I suppose we said the right thing about being Christians. We must remember to pray for him and for his son. This might be just the opportunity his boy has been waiting for."

"I'm sure we did the right thing," agreed Peter. "I felt a bit mean, though, sitting there listening to him telling us how they looked for mines, when all the time we are hoping like mad they won't find the one *we're* looking for. Finding a mine certainly seems a bit harder than I should have thought. They may not find it so soon after all—if they do find it at all. But then, neither may we. One thing I forgot to do was to ask him whose land this is.

Perhaps it was just as well, as he might have guessed we were up to something. It shouldn't be too hard to find out, though."

"Let's get a shift-on, Peter. We must get to Hasslow Dale before it rains. We can probably find some shelter there. It was stupid of us not to have brought macs, but it looked so jolly fine when we left."

As Tim spoke, a muffled roll of thunder broke the air. The sky had closed in about them, and the air seemed heavy and hard to breathe.

"Phew!" Peter exclaimed as they stood listening to the peal fade away. "We're going to get caught properly if we don't hurry. I don't fancy being caught out in the open like this in a thunder storm."

As they ran on it got darker all the time. The far hills had already disappeared under heavy cloud, rolling on like a relentless wave. Soon it seemed as though it was almost night, and all was silent except for the sound of the wind in the heather, the boys' shoes pounding on the ground, and their panting breath. The birds that had been singing earlier had stopped, and all was set for a really heavy storm. Through the blackness an old building stood out, like a beacon beckoning them to it. Being on the top of a rise, it stood out in a startling way.

"Let's make for that house, Peter," said Tim, his breath catching in the back of his throat as he drew it in.

"Right-ho, Tim. It's funny, though; from back

there it looked like a ruin but I can see now it's a proper house."

They still had a couple of hundred yards to go when the rain started—large drops falling, beating down on the boys. The house was not very big but of a rather peculiar design. It looked the sort of house that Hansel and Gretel might have found when they were lost in the woods.

"Perhaps there's a witch at home," panted Peter. "Let's hope we get a better reception than an oven. I wonder who lives here all on their own."

The rain was very heavy and they were both wet through when they reached the house. They went just inside the half-open door before knocking. On the door was a large knocker which Tim lifted and let fall. The result was far from what they expected. Instead of making an ordinary noise, it fell with a crash—a crash which seemed to fill the house, which seemed to echo everywhere, which seemed to fill their heads as though they would burst.

"Enough to wake the dead," whispered Peter, awed.

In the silence that followed, someone could be heard shuffling forwards. In the gloom, Peter could make out the shape of an old man tottering across the room.

"Who is it?" he croaked. "And what do you want? Don't come here trying to cause trouble."

"We're two boys and we want to shelter from the storm, if we may," said Peter, who had backed outside again.

"Well, don't stand there; come in," said the old man sharply.

The room was icy cold and they shivered involuntarily as they stepped in.

"I'll get a light," the old man muttered, and he disappeared into another room.

Peter and Tim looked around and took stock of the room. It was furnished in a fairly ordinary way, with a large, black range that was dead. The ceiling was low and dirty. There was a musty smell about the place. Neither boy said anything.

After a minute, their host returned with an oil lamp. In the glow, Peter could see the old man's features. The face had a wild, hunted look about it, and the eyes showed an unusual amount of white. Peter froze in his chair. After a moment, the old man turned to move some things on the table, and Peter pulled a stub of pencil and a piece of paper from his pocket and wrote two words on it. He slipped it across to Tim, who quickly looked at it. 'Mad Sam', he read.

He gasped, but his gasp was drowned by a roar of thunder that seemed to come from directly overhead, almost deafening them, and threatening to bring the house down.

Chapter 6

A QUESTION OF HUMOURING

"Don't you find it lonely up here?" asked Tim.

The old man had introduced himself and, as Peter had guessed, he was Mad Sam. After a few minutes' talking he had become quite friendly. There was, however, something very strange about him that made the boys wary. At Tim's question he looked rather sad.

"You see," he said, "I really have to live on my own because all the people in the village are mad. You understand no one could live in a community of mad people."

Peter remembered reading somewhere that often people who are insane think everyone else is mad. That settled the matter as far as he was concerned, but he and Tim were still in the house, and as long as they remained there it would be best to humour him. Peter therefore said how sorry he was that Mad Sam had had to move on account of the villagers.

"Yes," the old man said, "I still miss company though, so I'm right glad you two young fellows have come to shelter from the storm."

Peter noticed tears in his eyes and felt sorry for him.

In order to continue the conversation, Tim decided to bring up the topic of the moor and the mining company. Before he had finished, he realised that he had said the wrong thing. Mad Sam's eyes opened even wider than they had been and he quivered all over.

"The mine!" he screamed. "That wretched mining company coming trespassing on my moor! I'll get them off, though; the thieves and scoundrels!"

"Is it your moor?" asked Peter pleasantly, hoping to please the man who appeared to be under the impression he owned the moor.

"Of course it's my moor," shouted Mad Sam, calming down somewhat.

"Just like a child," thought Peter. "Pretending that everything's his."

But he was wrong.

"They've tried to take it away from me," the old man continued. "Aye, but it'll take more than a few to take it away from me. This moor's mine, and it'll be mine for ever." He thought for a minute and then whispered, "Come with me and I'll show you something."

He then signalled them to follow him into another room. Peter looked at Tim and pulled a face. Neither was quite sure what to do, and while they stood wondering Mad Sam turned round and said :

"Come on, will yer!"

Without hesitating, they both followed.

He led them into the next room and up an old flight of stairs built into the wall. On reaching the top, he paused to get his breath back.

"I'm not used to this," he wheezed. "I'm an old

man now, and I have to live downstairs all the time."

Neither Tim nor Peter knew what to say, so they kept quiet. After a moment he opened a door on the landing where they stood, and he went inside. The boys could see that the room was unfurnished, with a low, sloping ceiling caused by the roof. The plaster was falling off the walls and the floor went up and down as they walked on it. In the corner was a small, black metal box with Mad Sam bending over it. Peter felt a thrill of excitement. Small, black metal boxes in old cottages were the sort of thing that thrilled him. Mad Sam took a key that was hanging round his neck and inserted it in the lock.

The old man opened the lid dramatically as though the box was full of gold. Inside, was a bundle of papers tied in a dirty, pink ribbon.

"Here," he said slowly, "are the deeds of the moor and this house, but the robbers will never take them from me. I guard them too well for that."

Fearing another outburst, Peter said, "Why, yes, I'm sure you do."

Once again the old man quietened down. Having looked at the deeds, they made their way down, groping for the rail of the rickety stairs.

They paused in the back room that was obviously being used as a combined kitchen and bedroom. The place was in a terrible mess and the smell was shocking.

Mad Sam must have been aware of this, for he

said, "I'm sorry about the mess but I can't get about enough to do much myself. Really, I just do the bare essentials such as washing up."

Peter glanced at a pile of dirty dishes in the sink and noticed Tim doing the same thing. They both smiled.

Mad Sam went on: "The house is getting in a dreadful state now and I'm not sure what's going to happen to it."

Both Peter and Tim felt very sorry for the old man, so they offered to do a few things to help him. The old man seemed pleased for he showed them where a broom and cleaning materials were.

"Now look," said Peter firmly, "you go and sit down for a bit, and we'll let you know when we've finished."

Mad Sam shuffled off, smiling and cooing to himself like a child.

"Phew!" said Tim, once he had gone. "Doesn't it smell vile in here! Still, we might as well earn our keep while the storm lasts. The first thing I'm going to do is to open the windows and let a bit of air in. I shouldn't think they've been opened for years."

They set to work with a will, pausing at intervals to talk.

"Fancy the moor being his," said Peter, washing the windows down with a cloth. "Phew! Aren't they dirty! I didn't believe him until he showed us the deeds. Judging by the map attached, he owned up as far as the river bed in Hasslow Dale, which means the whole mine must be on his land.

So if we make a good job of this he might let us dig it out."

The job took longer than they thought it would, and Mad Sam seemed suspicious of them, for occasionally they would turn and find him standing in the doorway watching them. They had swept out thoroughly and even washed the stone floor. The windows and woodwork had been washed down and the room showed great improvement.

"The place really needs a coat of paint," said Tim. "But we've done the best we can, so let's go and find the old boy."

Mad Sam was really pleased at the job Peter and Tim had done, and he was near to crying.

"I don't know how to repay you both," he said shakily. "You're the first people who have ever been kind to me. I'd like to give you each a present but I've nothing to give. I get a pension but there's nothing left out of that at the end of the week."

"Look," said Peter, "there is one favour that we'd like you to do us—not as a reward for what we've done, because we did that to pay you back for the shelter; we'd like to have permission to look for Dragon's Claw Mine which we think is on your land."

Peter paused and swallowed hard, wondering what the old man's reaction would be to this. For a moment he looked as though he was going into another fit, but he smiled in a peculiar way.

"And what, may I ask, do you want with Dragon's Claw Mine?"

"We're interested in caves and caving," explained Peter hurriedly, "and any form of underground exploring. We heard about this lost mine and decided it would be exciting to find it and explore it. Of course, if you don't want . . ."

Peter, lost for words, let his voice trail away. Mad Sam looked very serious.

"The mine is certainly lost," he said. "I don't think you'll ever find it."

Having learnt from previous experience with the station master and Tom, Peter decided against asking why they would never find it and let the man continue.

"There's been many people looking for it in the past. Too many in fact, and they've all found nothing. I reckon the mine will keep its mystery for ever."

This was too much for Tim, who burst out, "What mystery is this?"

"Let them that finds it discover for themselves," replied Mad Sam mysteriously. "I don't think there's much chance of that, though; its Keepers guard it too well. Now then, if I were to give you permission, would you be wanting to work it for minerals?"

"Oh no!" exclaimed Peter. "We only want to have the fun of exploring it."

"Well, then, I'll tell you what I'll do. You find the mine and you can explore it. All the same, there's one condition attached to all this. I want no one else to know you've found it or they'll be wanting to mine it, and on no account must it be mined again."

All this mystery and the smell of the house was too much for the two boys, who said they had better be going. The sun was shining, and in comparison with the house it was very hot outside. They bade the old man good-bye and promised to call again.

"Quite a decent, old boy, provided one says the right thing—but quite mad!"

Tim voiced his opinion before they were properly out of the gate.

"Sssh!" said Peter. "He might hear and shoot us from one of the windows, with a blunderbuss. I agree, though, he's not really bad. You know, when he wanted to give us a present out of his pension, it brought a lump to my throat. I'd like to have tackled him further about the mine, but I thought I'd better not. Perhaps next time we call we could ask him. He'll have got to trust us better and might tell us more. All that talk about keepers and mystery!"

Tim agreed. "It made me creep, too. We must ask him what he meant, later. Crumbs! Do you realise what time it is? It's two o'clock. We've to be back by five, so let's have our lunch now and hurry on. I don't suppose we'll have much time at the mine."

They reached the valley and had a hurried lunch.

Peter pulled the old print carefully out of his bag. Although they could have drawn it from memory by this time, they still wanted to look at it.

"The valley's about three hundred and fifty

feet deep here," said Peter, "and the mine is just about half way down. That makes it about this level."

There were numerous sheep tracks running along the grassy hillside, so they split up, walking parallel to the bottom and within calling distance of each other. Peter felt discouraged. He had imagined rocks and miniature cliffs which would be the ideal setting for a mystery mine. In actual fact, the hillside was smooth except for the occasional stunted hawthorn tree. In complete contrast, the other side was rocky and heavily wooded. Deep in thought, Peter hardly heard Tim calling him.

"What did you say?" he shouted back.

"I asked if you'd found anything yet," Tim replied.

"No, not yet; and I don't think I will. Have you?"

"I don't know. Come up and look at this."

Peter clambered up the slope on all fours. Tim was standing by a hawthorn tree looking at a series of rabbit holes.

"I thought," he explained, "that the rabbits might have found a space behind that they were using."

"I doubt it," said Peter. "It would probably be too big and damp if it were the mine. Let's have another look at the tracing."

It was here that they noticed something which they had missed before. A large tree was shown on the top of the hill, directly above the mine. Although they must have seen it often enough they had failed to notice its significance.

"In that case all we'll have to do," said Peter, "is to climb to the top, find the tree and come straight down again. It's absolutely foolproof. Unless, of course," he added as an afterthought, "it was drawn by the artist for decoration. That's a risk we'll have to take."

They scrambled up the hill to find that there was further to go than they had thought. Each time it looked as though they had reached the top, the hill continued at a shallower angle until they almost despaired of reaching it.

"If we go on at this rate," said Tim, "we'll be in the clouds."

A stone wall marked the top, and the sight of it made even Peter stop grumbling about wasted energy. They looked in vain both ways for the tree. Only a few, miserable hawthorns broke the view.

"Magnificent tree," said Peter dryly. "I think it's worth a photograph."

Tim was trying to work out a puzzle. Something did not seem quite right. Then it dawned on him.

"We're complete asses," he enlightened Peter. "That print must be well over a hundred years old."

"So what?" retorted Peter. "I imagine they could see as well then as we can today."

"I know that, but I meant that it was unlikely the tree would be here now."

"I've got it!" shouted Peter. "What we've got to look for is a stump and not a tree. Brilliant."

"Exactly," said Tim, who immediately started

running alongside the wall. Peter followed on the opposite side and found the stump almost at once

"Here it is," he called out. "It's massive enough to be it, anyway."

Peter's idea of massive was evidently not Tim's, but they set off slipping and sliding downhill.

"We must stop at the first likely thing we come to, Tim," Peter said.

About halfway down, in the expected place, they found an old hawthorn and a short scree slope. From that point downwards, the hill showed signs of wear as though water or stones had descended there at some time.

"I guess this is it," said Peter. "Whoever would have thought of looking behind a scree slope? There are so many of these patches of small stones around here, and they make a perfect camouflage. Come on; let's investigate."

They started to pull the stones away with their bare hands. One largish one rolled down the hill before they could stop it. They watched it gathering speed, bouncing as it went. On the opposite bank, a fisherman was quietly dozing with his rod resting beside him. As it reached the bottom, the stone gave one magnificent leap and landed with a loud splash in the river. Evidently under the impression that he had caught a large salmon, the fisherman leapt into action. Finding nothing on the end of his line, he must have become suspicious, for he looked up the hill and, seeing the two boys laughing, waved his arms angrily and shouted. Tim was in favour of running away but Peter pointed out that there was not much danger as the river presented quite an obstacle.

Tim noticed that the time was short if they were to return and get cleaned up in time for tea with the Parkinsons. The clouds were returning again, and they decided to leave the mine alone for the day. They hurried back the short way, down the valley, but even so they were slightly late for tea.

"Don't worry," said Mrs. Parkinson when they apologised. "We weren't expecting you too early from what we know of young people. I think we'll start tea straight away if that's all right with you."

Peter and Tim, who were starving, assured her that it was. The vicar said grace, and the boys tucked in.

"Tell me," he said, "what sort of a day have you had? Did you have any luck?"

"We had a most amazing day," replied Peter, hastily emptying his mouth. "At the end of it we discovered the mine."

"Peter," said Tim quietly and slowly, "I've been thinking and I'm not so sure that we have. You see, there's no road up to the place we've found as the print shows there should be, and there never could have been: the hill's much too steep!"

Chapter 7

TALES OF THE UNSEEN

"Isn't it dark!" exclaimed Mrs. Parkinson. "I think we'd better have the lights on. I do believe there's going to be another storm."

Having finished tea, they had all retired to the sitting-room and were talking about things in general. After Tim's startling announcement, it was hardly surprising that the topic of the mine should be brought up again.

"Tell me," said the vicar, leaning forward in his armchair. "Supposing you haven't found the mine, is there any chance of finding it?"

Peter and Tim were both puzzled by the point of the road that they had completely overlooked. Peter answered.

"I suppose if the place we've found isn't the mine, then it's a write-off. But it *must* be it. Anyway, we're jolly well going to dig it out."

"Where is this place?" asked the vicar.

Tim was about to answer but Peter shook his head. "I'm afraid we can't tell you; we've been sworn to secrecy."

"Really? If it's not being too nosey, may I ask who by?"

Mr. Parkinson could not conceal his interest in the matter, for he, too, had heard of all the mystery attached to the mine.

"Actually, it was the owner of the land," explained Tim.

At this the vicar was really startled. "What, old Mad Sam?" he asked.

"I say, do you know him?" asked Tim.

"Well, put it this way: I know about him. I'm afraid that I have something to confess to you," said the vicar, laughing.

The boys looked interested but said nothing. He continued:

"When you told me about the mine, I decided to do a bit of investigating on my own. I've found out one or two very interesting things. Perhaps you'd like to hear them."

Peter and Tim nodded violently.

"Well, firstly, I found it very difficult to get anyone to talk. As soon as I mentioned the subject, they shut up like clams. However, you often find that people will confide in a clergyman when they won't trust anyone else. Naturally, I didn't press the point, but as I had one or two visits to make I brought up the matter in the course of conversation. At last I found one dear, old lady who was quite willing to talk. Indeed, it was hard to get her to stop. Her grandfather had evidently mined there just before it was closed. She remembers being told about it by him when she was small.

"The main body of the villagers are against it being worked as they have a legend which you probably know about—the one that says working the mine will bring death to the village."

Tim nodded.

"Right. Now, as far as I can gather, throughout its history no one has been very keen on working it. It was supposed to be cursed and an evil spirit was said to haunt it. About 1840 the climax came. The hauntings were supposed to have increased and the miners refused to work. They held out against their employers for some time, but money ran short and their families suffered in consequence. Some went farther afield to Castleton where there was a limited amount of employment in mines. One or two, however, decided to brave the horrors of the mine and go back. I must emphasise that only a few went back, and the rest set on these and attacked them. Why, I can't imagine. The few who had returned evidently did so against their better judgment, goaded on by a promised increase in pay.

"At that time, the cottage where Mad Sam lives on the moor was occupied by a woman who was supposed to be a witch. She definitely had a crystal ball and claimed to be able to tell the future. She was feared by the villagers and they respected her. She warned the miners against returning, saying the mine wanted to be left alone and would take the next intruders as prisoners—typical olden day superstition. As was quite often the case in those days, the mine, which was partly a natural cave, was supposed to reach right down to the underworld. A dog was found there after being lost for about two weeks. To put it in the words of the old lady who told me, 'His eyes were put out and his coat burnt to a cinder'. Probably what happened

was that the dog, panicking when it realised it was
lost, ran about colliding with walls and rocks till
it skinned and blinded itself.

"Now we come to the peculiar part of the story.
One miner who wasn't superstitious went in alone
to see just what the state of the lead supply was.
He never returned. The villagers presumed the
mine had taken him. The mine owners, trying to
prove there was nothing wrong with the mine,
volunteered to work it for a bit by themselves. The
miners wouldn't even agree to this, but, taking
tools, the owners went in before they could be
stopped. A few hours later, a massive explosion
shook the village, bringing the people running out
of their houses in terror. Of course, they all knew
what had happened: the mine had claimed some
more victims. The villagers wanted to close the
mine at once but the dead people's relatives at
least wanted the bodies back. The locals said there
would be none, but because of a code among
miners a search had to be made and a party went
in and found the owners dead.

"Actually, in the past there were minor earth-
quakes at odd intervals which used to bring down
parts of the mine, but these have stopped since it
has ceased to be worked. What had evidently happened this time was that the rock where they had
been was in a state that makes it explode when
hammered. There was an explosion of the same
type, about a hundred years before, at nearby
Eyam. The rock is called slickenside. Naturally, all
this, coupled with the witch's story, was too much

for the village, and the entrance was sealed and all records of the mine destroyed. The people of that day never revealed where it was and no one knows where it is today, although you seem to have discovered a clue to its whereabouts."

The vicar leaned back and let the boys think it over. It was Peter who broke the silence, almost making the others jump, so absorbed had they all become with the story.

"Where does Mad Sam come into the picture?" he asked. "I can't make it out at all. He said he didn't want the mine worked, and yet he's given permission to a mining company to look for it. It doesn't make sense but I suppose that's just part of his madness."

"Haven't you heard about that?" asked the vicar, looking surprised.

"No. What's happened?" Tim was interested.

"Well, some time ago, this mineral company wanted to look for minerals, and Mad Sam's father leased the mineral rights for about a hundred years. Mad Sam comes from a big farming family, and most of the moor is his. Now Mad Sam wants the mineral rights back but of course he can't get them. The company that rented the mineral rights is the same one that's working now. They've only just started—since your uncle went away."

"So that's why Uncle Jack didn't mention it," reflected Peter. "I wondered why he hadn't warned us not to be too open in our search."

"You seem to have found out more than we have," said Tim. "All we knew was that the mine was lost and it was supposed to have half a mile of workings. Still, there are one or two points you haven't cleared up. You haven't said how it got its name or why people don't want it found today. There is a rumour going that working it will bring death to the village."

"Another thing," said Peter. "Mad Sam said he supposed the Keepers of the mine would preserve its mystery and secret for ever. What on earth are its Keepers and what is this secret?"

"Woa!" said the vicar, and he laughed. "One question at a time. I know the answer to Tim's two questions but not Peter's. The mine was called Dragon's Claw Mine because, after the explosion in the mine, the rescue party found, just above the bodies, a mark on the wall which they said looked like a dragon's claw. I forgot to mention that; I'm sorry. That was one of the things that helped to close the mine. This marking must be some peculiarity of the rock in the mine because it was found quite often after blasting, but this one was the largest claw ever found. I don't know when the name actually came into use, but it must have been some time before the mine was closed.

"Now, about this rumour. The only explanation I can think of is that at the back of the villagers' minds is still an inbred fear of the mine, although they don't know exactly what to fear. Because of this, they seize on the first thing they can think of to justify their fear, and death seemed quite good, so it stuck. It is amazing, really, what a large amount of superstition there is about even nowadays, especially in the country. I might be wrong, of course. There could easily be some other explanation. There might really be a threat to the village. I just can't think what the secret of the mine's Keepers is; my information didn't include that point."

"I see," said Peter. "That's terrific! It covers just about everything."

"Oh, no, it doesn't," said the vicar. "I've told you my bit; now it's your turn. Tell me about your meeting with Mad Sam."

Peter and Tim together told him the story of their strange meeting in the thunderstorm and their attempts to find the mine. They carefully omitted telling the vicar of the site and explained why they did so.

"Perhaps," finished Peter, "one day Mad Sam will give us permission to tell other people but, until he does, mum's the word. I think it would be best really if no one else knew we were even looking for it, or we might run into trouble with the villagers."

They talked until quite late that night, and the two boys were feeling sleepy when they left the vicarage and made their way back to the coach-house. As they got to the loft Peter said:

"Come on; let's have Q.T. and get straight to bed so we can have a really early start in the morning. Then we can begin digging before anyone else . . . Are you listening, Tim?"

"Mmmmm?"

"I said, are you listening?"

"To what? I can't hear anything."

"To me, saying let's get to bed early and . . . Oh, never mind. What *are* you doing?"

"I'm looking at this old print of yours. I've just noticed that the thing we thought was a road isn't a road at all. It's a kind of a railway running up the hill. I imagine it was for lowering lead or something."

"Let's have a look," said Peter, waking up. "Yes, you're right."

"Of course I'm right," protested Tim, pretending to be offended. "You didn't think I'd be wrong, did you?"

"Quite frankly—yes. I couldn't see how a horse and cart could come down a railway, but I can see now that the horse and cart is on a road that joins the railway. These kinds of prints aren't very clear. All sorts of scratchy lines. However, that solves the problem of the missing road. Now all we have to do is to find the house by the side of the mine."

Tim yawned and put the print down. "I think we can assume that that's artist's imagination. Come on; let's have Q.T. and get to bed so that we can have a really early start in the morning."

Peter was too tired to tell his friend that that was what he'd been trying to tell him for some time.

Chapter 8

UNTIL THEY COME TO SOMETHING

As they tramped across the moor, the early morning mist was still on the ground, giving a pleasant, unreal appearance. The storm appeared to have blown itself out during the night and everything was fresh. The turf squelched in places as they walked on it.

"It's lucky we've got boots on," exclaimed Tim, noticing how wet it was underfoot. He paused for a minute and sighed. "Here you are, lazy; it's your turn now." He slipped the rucksack from his back and let Peter put it on. "After all," he continued, "you wanted to bring the beastly stuff."

By 'beastly stuff', he meant the equipment Peter had insisted on bringing. There was a spade with a short handle. (The short handle was Tim's suggestion; it would fit into the rucksack and would not attract attention.) Then there was a crowbar to remove any large stones, a rope, and small items such as a torch, a camera and lunch.

Tim had been just as keen to bring the stuff as Peter; but although Peter realised this he remained tactfully quiet. The morning was too new and peaceful to start an argument, even a friendly one.

With no hindrances, they soon reached the side

of the valley above the site they wanted to excavate, and Tim looked at his watch.

"It's half past seven," he announced, "so if we start digging straight away we'll have an hour and a half to dig before anybody's likely to be around. I shouldn't think anybody'll be here before nine, would you?"

Peter shook his head and went sliding down the hill on the wet, dewy grass. When they reached the hawthorn tree, it was so slippery that they had difficulty in stopping.

"You can see where the railway ran down," said Peter.

The hill was worn, and the day before they had taken it for a track or watercourse where water ran down in very wet weather.

"No sign of the house, though, Tim. I reckon we can forget about that."

They turned their attention to the area of small stones about five feet in diameter, wondering what strange secret was lurking behind them.

Standing dreaming, Peter did not notice Tim unpacking, and it was not until he received a lump of earth on the back of his head that he became aware of what was going on around him.

"Come on, dreamy," said Tim. "You don't think I'm going to dig this lot out on my own, do you?"

"Not really," replied Peter calmly. "Anyway, what are we going to do with all this small stone? We can't shovel it down the hill or people will notice it. I should think it would be best if we put it all on this flat bit above, and then, if we want to close it, all we have to do is to push it down again."

Tim picked up the crowbar and plunged it into the stones. It sank a few inches and then stopped dead. He tried in another place and the same thing happened.

"Well," he said, standing to one side, "it seems we might be on to something. It's rock and not earth behind."

They took it in turns to dig the stones away, throwing them on the shallow slope above. After digging for nearly an hour, they exposed a large slab of limestone.

"I guess that's the thing that's sealing the mine," said Peter. "They used to do it with tombs ages ago. I remember reading about it."

Tim laughed. "There's no need to be so cheerful. This isn't a tomb, is it?"

Peter said nothing, and he thought this over. Although the early morning sun was streaming down the valley, he couldn't help giving a shiver. "I've been up too late listening to the vicar's tales," he thought. He soon forgot about it as they set to to remove the large slab of rock.

They dug away behind so that they could put the bar in and lever. When all was ready they both leaned on the bar. What happened then surprised them both. Instead of coming away from the hill, the stone swung in the ground, as though on a central pivot. Leaving it as it was, they inspected the slab further and found that it actually was on a pivot. It was set in a framework of stone blocks

and was supported on rusty iron pegs, top and
bottom, on which it swung. At this stage, a wave
of cold air surged out of the hole, and at once the
boys realised they had found the mine. The cold
air and the smell were both familiar to them, as
they exist in almost every cave or place underground.

They stood and looked; then Peter said, "Come
on; what are we waiting for? Let's go in!"

Tim was more cautious and wanted to conceal
their tracks a bit.

"Hang on a moment; let's get all our kit inside
and squash the new earth down a bit so it doesn't
look as though we've been digging; then we can
close the rock behind us."

"Right," agreed Peter. "It's amazing they should
have made it so easy to get into. I imagined it
would be permanently sealed."

They shone a torch inside but their eyes were
not adjusted to the darkness and they could not see
far. Making sure that there was level ground and
not a shaft just inside the opening, they squeezed
in and pulled their kit in behind them. Switching
on the torch, they closed the rock.

After a few moments their eyes got accustomed
to the darkness and they looked around them. The
passage they were in was about two and a half feet
wide and five feet high. At the entrance the height
was a lot less. To their dismay, the way ahead was
barred by more rock. They searched for any possible way past but had to admit defeat.

"It can't be much," said Peter, trying to be

cheerful, "or else the draught wouldn't be able to get by. Let's try and dig it away."

"Well for goodness sake be careful," said Tim, who was worried. "It may be a roof-fall, and we'll have the whole lot down on top of us if we disturb it any further."

Peter picked up the crowbar. "It's okay, Tim. I've looked at the roof. It's sound enough. This is just rock piled up, presumably to bar the way. We're not in as easily as we thought."

For two hours or more they struggled to remove the rock and their hands were torn about by the limestone. Pulling one large piece away, Peter could see the way beyond. With a bit more work and a very tight squeeze they forced their way through. Shining their light down the passage, the way looked free.

On the floor was a yellowish, slushy mud, and underneath they could feel rails. The floor dipped and so did the roof. Crouching low, they emerged on the other side to find the passage was rising steadily. Here the floor was free from the yellow mud and they could see the rusted rails clearly. These all but touched the passage sides, and the trucks must have filled the width of it completely.

"I guess you had to be pretty nifty on your feet," laughed Tim, "when a truck came whistling down the slope."

"I imagine these niches in the wall are to get into," said Peter. "After all, you'd get a fair amount of warning and they're placed every few yards."

"I hadn't really noticed them. I thought they were just places where the miners had worked for lead, but I expect you're right. It seems a reasonble explanation, anyway."

They pressed on and soon the passage levelled out. After something like a hundred feet it split into two, with one passage going left and the other straight on. At this point they noticed that the passage going straight on widened and also got higher. Shining their torch down each one in turn they decided on the large one. In this the rails continued and the going was easy.

After going some way they paused to discuss what they should do. After the clanging of their nailed boots against the rock and the rails, everything seemed very quiet. At intervals the silence was broken by water dripping from the roof making a chinking sound as it hit the floor.

They stood still for a moment, thinking where they were and what they had done. Here, with about one hundred and fifty feet of limestone over their heads, were two schoolboys who had found a mine that had not been entered for well over a hundred years. As they stood listening to the water dripping, they realised how fortunate they were. If they hadn't looked in that old junk-shop and spotted that print, they wouldn't be here now; but they had and they were. Too much so, in fact, thought Peter, as a large, cold drop of water went down his neck.

"I'm not going to stand here for ever," he said. "The thing is, are we going to go on or turn back!

Whatever we do, we oughtn't to take long as we've
only one torch and, apart from the risk of its running out, the bulb might go. This calls for proper
lamps and equipment."

"Oh!" exclaimed Tim. "I couldn't turn back
now. I've got the fever of exploration! Let's go on
a bit more until we come to something definite."

"*You* don't want to go back!" cried Peter.
"What do you think *I* want to do—leave the mine
for ever? I only suggested we went back because
it would be safer. You know perfectly well our
school Club wouldn't allow an expedition on one
torch and no spares." Peter grinned. "I agree
though it would be cruel to turn back now. Let's
go on, as you say, until we come to something."

The 'something' was not far away. The passage
turned slightly right and dipped. In the middle
of the dip the floor of the passage simply did not
exist, but the rails continued over a bridge made
of wood. The gap was only about eight feet across
but, not knowing how deep it was, the boys
approached cautiously. Stopping a few feet away
Tim picked up a stone and threw it down. It hit
the side and, after a pause, went to the bottom
with a splash.

Tim looked at Peter. "Water!" he said, not so
much to tell Peter but as an exclamation.

Standing up rather unsteadily, Tim walked to
the bridge and started to get on it.

"Get off!" Peter shouted.

Tim jumped at the sudden noise and nearly fell
down the pit.

"I wish you wouldn't shout," he said. "It's bad or the nerves."

Peter ignored this last remark. "Never trust a wooden thing underground," he explained. "Wood rots terribly quickly in a damp atmosphere, and the bridge might easily give way."

"How can we test it, then?" asked Tim, realising his mistake.

"I don't think we can, really. We'll just have to put a rope across and make the crossing singly. I suppose we could hurl one of these rocks on but, even if the bridge didn't break, I wouldn't trust it. Come on; we've found our 'something', so let's get back. I feel famished, anyway."

Peter was really feeling rather worried. Being in a strange mine without proper equipment did not appeal to him. When they came back with proper equipment, things would be different.

They made their way out fairly quickly, to find that the sun was shining brightly. As they stood blinking in the sunlight a dog barked in the distance. This was the only sound to disturb the silence—a silence different from that of underground, a silence of life not of death.

They took a short rest, had a swig of water and moved off. Tim glanced at his watch and was surprised to see how late it was.

"It's half past eleven," he told Peter. "We might as well have lunch back at the Vicarage, so there's no need to hurry back. Let's go over the moor and see how our quarrying friends are getting on. We'll cautiously ask them if they've found anything yet."

F

"Yes, and offer our advice for a small fee."

"It would be rather fun," reflected Tim, "if they found another entrance and we met half way."

For a long time they walked in silence, taking in the beauty of the moor. The bees buzzed in the heather, and the birds chirped and twittered all round them. High in the cloudless sky, a hawk circled ceaselessly looking for prey, ignoring the crows that flapped backwards and forwards in an endless chain. All this was too much for Peter, who lay down at the top of a high bank above the track used by vehicles going over the moor.

"What's up?" asked Tim.

"Just sit down a moment and look round. Don't you think it's wonderful. It makes me wonder why we go underground. It can only be for adventure. Most people think it's for the beauty of the formations, but they're dead and all this is living. What a wonderful and yet amazing thing life is. I could lie here for ever."

"I fear," said Tim, with a piece of grass between his lips, "that you're getting over sentimental. But I suppose I feel the same way. . . . *What's that?*"

Tim and Peter leapt to their feet. Fairly close at hand came a screeching of brakes and a scrunching sound of wheels skidding on the gravel of the road.

Chapter 9

HIDE-AND-SEEK

About fifty yards down the road, with a cloud of dust blowing from under its wheels, was a Land Rover. The occupant was climbing out, and they recognised him as the surveyor they had talked to the previous day when they were nearly attacked by the workmen. On the left of the vehicle lay a bundle of clothing as though someone was huddled on the grass.

As the surveyor bent down to inspect it, a figure detached itself from a heap of gravel on the opposite side of the road. It was a man with a handkerchief over his mouth, and he crept swiftly towards the door of the Land Rover. The boys stood and stared as he opened the door and pulled out a brief-case. Suddenly Peter came to life.

"Quick," he said; "get the camera out and we'll have a photograph. You run along the top of the bank and photograph downwards while I run along the road. He may not see you then. I'll try to get his mask off so that the police will be able to recognise him."

Tim ran swiftly across the top while Peter shouted down the road.

"Look out!" he cried.

The man was obviously startled and hesitated

for a moment. In the second that he hesitated, the surveyor spun round and made straight for the man. He aimed a blow at the man's face but he dodged it. In the fight that followed, the mask was dislodged and the man dropped the brief-case. Tim, at the top of the bank, took two or three photographs.

The surveyor took a step backwards and tripped on the verge. The man took advantage of the surveyor stumbling and hit him a really hard blow. With a groan, the surveyor dropped to the ground and the attacker stood panting. Peter did not know what to do. He did not wish to get caught, but he did want Tim to get away. Tim, however, was still taking photographs. Leaning forward, he almost overbalanced, then righted himself, but as he did so the earth under his feet gave way and he rolled down the bank.

The man saw the camera and lunged at Tim who was picking himself up. Tim saw him coming and dodged out of the way. Peter was manoeuvring himself round behind the man and Tim pretended not to have noticed.

"Give me the camera," ordered the man.

"No."

"I said, give me the camera. If you don't, you little wretch, you'd better hold yourself responsible for anything that happens to you."

Tim just stood and looked at him. The man moved menacingly towards him. Tim held tight onto the camera, and Peter signed to Tim to throw it. Just as the man was about to grab him, Tim threw the camera to Peter. Peter caught it neatly and started running. The man was lost, for the moment, as to what had happened. When he saw Peter running, he went straight up to Tim and gave him a blow on the face. Tim fell over backwards. Turning, without another look at Tim, the man ran after Peter who was running hard some distance ahead.

Peter turned and noticed Tim lying still and the man following close behind. He put on an extra burst of speed and wondered where to make for. There were no buildings around and it looked as though he was in for a long run. Suddenly he remembered the small mine he and Tim had passed the day before. If only he could get over the rise in time so that he could enter without being seen! If only he could last out! If only . . . *Crash!* Peter tripped in a rabbit hole and fell flying forward. Everything went white, then black and, for a few moments, very peaceful. He quickly came to his senses, got up and started off again. "Lucky my ankle's not twisted," he thought.

He turned round again and was surprised to see how close the man was to him. Although he had lain there for only a few seconds, those seconds had made a lot of difference. Peter spotted the bushes round the mine a few hundred yards away. His breath was coming jerkily and he could hear the man pounding along behind. For a moment he felt as though he could not go a step further. His legs felt heavy and weak up the back of the knees, and he wanted to give himself up.

When he reached the mine he had gained quite a bit of ground and he decided to take the chance and go inside. Panting, he squeezed between the two boulders that blocked the entrance and stumbled inside. He felt in his two pockets for a light and was relieved to find he still had the torch he had put there after they had come out of Dragon's Claw Mine. Half crouching, he stumbled on, knocking his head once or twice on the uneven roof. Reaching some water, he waded straight through, without hesitating, and got to the top of the shaft. The passage continued for a bit beyond, and Peter jumped across.

He stood listening for any sounds of his being followed. To his horror, he heard shouting at the far end of the passage. The words were indistinct but he realised that he was concerned.

"Oh God," he said, the words choking in his mouth, "please don't let him catch me."

He lowered his head, and as he raised it his eyes caught sight of another passage he had forgotten about. In the top of the roof was a small opening, running back overhead and only visible from his side of the shaft, and even then not easily.

As he looked for a foothold he heard water being splashed up in the passage behind him. With new energy given by his fear he scrabbled into the hole, skinning his legs in the process. It was only a small hole and it went back about four feet. Squeezed inside it, Peter was just about to switch his torch out when he had the idea of removing the film from the camera. In this way, even if the camera was taken from him, he would still have the film. As he was afraid of his light being seen, he took the film out in the darkness. He then placed the film in his back trouser pocket.

The footsteps were approaching closer now and the man was shouting to him to give up. There was a pause and then the sound of a match being struck. "So that's how he's getting his light," thought Peter. The man must have reached the shaft because he could be heard throwing stones down it.

"If you're down there you'd better call out," he shouted fiercely, "'cos I'm going to roll a big rock down."

Trembling all over, Peter lay and thought. Surely the man would hear his heart beating. It was pounding away, amplified by the confined space, until it sounded like a hammer mill. Surely the man would guess where he was! Surely . . . Crash! The rock had been rolled down the hole exactly as the man had threatened.

"Thank the Lord I'm not down there," breathed Peter, and he was indeed thanking God in his heart.

There was a long period of silence in which the man could be heard breathing heavily. Peter's head was spinning round as he lay in the hole. "Just like hide-and-seek," he thought, "only the man didn't count a hundred before coming to look for me. What a horrible game this is. I can't give myself up and the man won't shout 'I give in'. I'll just have to lie here until he goes or until . . . I wonder what's happened to Tim and the surveyor. What was his name? Mr. Wheeler, I think. He might have gone for help with Tim. Even if he has, he won't know where we are. The moor could be surrounded, I suppose. That would take time, though. Let me see, the nearest towns with any-thing like a police force are Bakewell and Buxton. Take them some time to get here. By that time I'll have been caught or left alone. Supposing no one comes to look for us at all? I can't stay here too long; it's too cramped."

Zippp! Another match being struck, a curse and the sound of footsteps fading away. Peter heard them splashing through water, another curse (pre-sumably the man had hit his head) and, finally, silence. This was too good to be true. It must be a trap. The man was just waiting for Peter to come out. He wouldn't. He'd stay there. But what a ghastly position to be in. He didn't know if the man had gone.

If he had, he was lying cramped for nothing when he could be away getting help. On the other hand, if it was a trap and he went out, well . . . He thought of hiding the film so that it would be safe if he were caught. No, that would be no good. If anything happened to him, the film would never be found.

How long he lay hidden he did not know. It seemed like hours, but it could not have been as long as that. The ideas and thoughts that had been racing round his head earlier had stopped, and he had only one object in mind—to get out. . . . To get out! What a fool he'd been, lying in that hole all the time. The man *must* have gone. The least he could do would be to get down quietly and see what was happening.

"Please, Lord," he prayed, "keep me safe. Don't let me be caught. Please help me to do the right thing."

As quietly as possible he slid out of the hole and fished around with his foot for a foothold. He found one and lowered himself slowly. Another handhold and he should be able to touch the ground with his other foot. No; where was it? It couldn't be far; he might as well drop the rest; there was only mud below. Thud! He dropped and there seemed to be no ground beneath. For one horrible moment he thought he had fallen down the shaft.

He lay on the ground, aware of a dull pain in one leg. He felt around and his hand touched a piece of clothing. Not his, surely! Terrified, he realised there was a limb inside it. Then it dawned on him what had happened. His leg had gone to sleep in the hole, and, when he put his weight on it, it had collapsed. He started to laugh with a deep shaking of his body and chest. He froze again. Surely that was a splash in the passage. Was he caught at last? He felt sick. One faint hope that it might be his rescuers was shattered when the person approaching called out.

"I thought I'd catch you if I hid. Thought I'd gone, didn't you?" he snarled.

Peter said nothing but withdrew as far as the

passage would allow. There were about five feet between him and the shaft. The man couldn't be far away.

Zippp! Another match was struck, sending out a stabbing glare that made Peter blink and turn his head away. Crouched against the rock, he could not have been very visible, for the man stood shielding the match, peering around in the flickering light. The light shining upwards lit only parts of the man's face, giving him a ghostly appearance. For the first time Peter could get a good look at the man who had tried to rob the surveyor. He was shabbily dressed in a blue suit and was unshaven. He looked strong, although gaunt. "Probably an escaped convict on the run," thought Peter, as a shiver ran down his spine. The feeling was coming back to his leg and it felt as though it would burst.

The man lit another match and suddenly noticed Peter.

"Okay," he snarled. "I've seen you. Come on; hand over the camera."

Peter thought quickly. If he handed over the camera, the man probably wouldn't notice the film had gone, but then he was hardly likely to let Peter go. On the other hand, if he didn't hand it over now he was caught. . . .Well! There was at least some hope if he handed it over but none if he didn't.

"Supposing I hand it over," asked Peter, trying to sound confident, "what will you do with me?"

"Give you a fair chance. You'll be tied up, but I expect you'll be found. If you don't hand it over, then I'll have to take it from you; and I warn you, boy, I won't guarantee your future happiness."

Although he sounded reasonably pleasant, Peter realised this was just part of his treachery. Picking up the camera, Peter tossed it to the man.

"That's the boy. Now let's have the film out that your bright friend took, and we'll burn it."

This was a situation Peter had not foreseen. The whole thing was over now. With his head throbbing and cheeks prickling, he waited while the man tore open the camera back.

"Clever, aren't you!" he snapped. "You thought I'd be fooled, but I wasn't."

"So it seems."

"You're going to pay for this."

With this, the man lit another match and started forward. What Peter did then often amazed him afterwards, and thinking about it in bed at night he would break out in a cold sweat. In the second that the man took to reach him, he worked out a plan. The shaft, he thought, was six feet across. The man would have to take a short run to jump it. Now, if he could cause the man to fall down, it would make a very efficient prison for, although only about twelve feet deep, the sides were smooth and slippery.

The man had backed for his run and Peter whipped the torch from his pocket and shone it in the man's face as he took off. The man staggered, tried to stop, flung himself forward and landed on Peter's side. Still blinded by the torch that Peter kept on, he swung his arms round to get his balance, forgetting he was in a confined place. His hands crashed against the jagged walls and he slipped into the shaft. Peter thought he had gone but the man still had hold of the edge of the shaft. There was only one thing to do. Remembering what he had done to Tim, Peter pushed the man's fingers from the edge. With a bellow the man let go, and Peter heard him hit the bottom with a thud.

Going to the edge Peter shone his torch down on the man, who was cursing and swearing.

"Comfortable?" he asked.

It was his turn now to ask the questions and give the orders. He dodged back as a stone was flung up at him.

"See you later," was all Peter said as he turned and made his way out. As he reached the fresh air he could have cried with relief. Here he was, free, when he ought to have been the prisoner. What a wonderful sensation. Things were better than he had prayed for. He tried to close the rocks at the entrance but all his strength seemed to have gone. Realising he could not do this, he made his way as quickly as possible back to the Land Rover, Tim and Mr. Wheeler.

As he climbed up to the top of the track he heard the motor revving up.

"Stop!" he shouted, "Stop!"

Someone must have heard, for the motor stopped; then Tim's head appeared at the top.

"Peter!" he exclaimed. "Are you all right? Where's the camera?"

"Oh, he took the camera, but I've got the film. He's fallen down the shaft in the mine we passed yesterday."

"Is he . . . is he . . . is he dead?" asked Tim apprehensively. After all, Peter had put things rather crudely.

"Dead! Far from it. Fighting fit!" He turned to Mr. Wheeler who was in the Land Rover. "Let's get to the nearest phone and ask for the police. It will take him some time to escape."

They set off as quickly as possible.

"Are you all right, Tim?" asked Peter. "He certainly hit you a wallop."

Tim laughed. "He didn't hit me hard, although it feels as though my chin's smashed to pulp," he said, rubbing it. "Mr. Wheeler was the one who got hit hard. He's only just come round properly. That's why we haven't got away for help before."

Mr. Wheeler turned to Peter. "I don't know how to thank you two. That man nearly got away with a thousand pounds in cash. I drew the money in the bank at Buxton and then I remembered I had a map to pick up here. The money is this week's wages for the firm, amongst other things. It was stupid of me not to have dropped the money into the office first, but I didn't really think it necessary. Anyway, when I got to our huts up there I took the brief-case with the money in it out of the car, mentioning it to the other surveyor. I noticed this other character hanging around; he must have overheard me. I asked him what he wanted and he said he was after work. When I told him I had none, he soon made off and I thought I'd seen the last of him."

"But how did he get you to stop in the road?" asked Peter.

"I'm coming to that. I was driving fairly fast, when I noticed something that looked like a body lying by the side of the road. Naturally I stopped to investigate, and, well, you know the rest better than I do. That man had put a coat over some stones, knowing I'd stop. It was very lucky for me that you were around. Your friend tells me that you have photographs, and now I gather you have even caught the man.

"Well, here's the phone box. I think it would be better if *I* spoke to the police."

The boys nodded and Mr. Wheeler went into the box.

"Oh Tim," said Peter when they were alone, "it was awful. I was alone with him in that mine. I'll tell you about it later."

They sat in silence, watching the surveyor through the glass door. He spoke for a few moments and then called to Peter.

"They want to know where he is," he said.

Feeling rather nervous, Peter picked up the phone and explained as clearly as possible to the police where the mine was.

That was a day the boys were not likely to forget. It did not take the police long to arrive, and a small army of them were swarming over the moor, led by Peter and Tim. The man was where Peter had left him, and he became very

violent when arrested. He was put in one of the
cars and driven away. An officer went up to the
surveyor.

"I'd like to thank you, sir, for assisting us in
catching that man. He escaped from prison about
ten days ago, and he has been on the run ever
since. We never expected him as far north as this."

"Good gracious, don't thank me," said the surveyor. "These two boys caught him. I only drove
them to the phone box."

Peter and Tim looked at the ground.

"We took some photographs of him fighting Mr.
Wheeler," said Peter, "but I don't imagine they'll
be much use now he's caught. Here's the film if
you want it; it's not much use to us."

The police officer took the film. "Don't be too
pessimistic," he said. "This will come in as valuable evidence at his trial. Robbery with violence,
you know. Well, anyway, thanks a lot. Good-bye. I
expect you'll be hearing from us later."

The police car accelerated in a cloud of dust.
As it disappeared, the surveyor turned to the boys.

"What about the camera?" he asked.

"I don't think it's much use now," replied Peter.
"It fell down the shaft with the man and there's
a lot of mud and water down there. It's still there,
in fact. Do you think the police would replace it?
It wasn't a very expensive one."

"Don't worry about it," said Mr. Wheeler. "I'd
like to have the pleasure of doing that. One each.
Now what kind was it?"

Peter and Tim protested that they wouldn't

dream of letting him replace it, but he insisted, so they told him the type.

"And film; what film do you use?"

"We were using fast panchromatic," said Peter, "as we were going to take some pictures underground . . . er, we're doing a spot of caving," he explained hurriedly, realising he might have put his foot in it.

"Well, well," said the surveyor. "Similar to my line."

"Yes," replied Peter, "very similar!"

Chapter 10

INTO THE UNKNOWN

"Come on, Peter. Do wake up! It's seven o'clock."

It was the morning after the hold-up episode and, although they had hoped for another really early start, they had slept well and woken up later than they had planned. When Tim awoke he was amazed to see what time it was. He leaned across and shook Peter. He actually expected quite a session getting his friend up, but much to Tim's surprise he leapt out of bed immediately and said,

"Well, come on. What are we waiting for?"

"Er, breakfast actually. I work better on a full stomach. I believe you do, too."

They washed, had breakfast and packed their much treasured kit. This time they were bringing all their equipment, as a full day's exploration was planned. Again the vicar called just as they were about to leave.

"Hello, Timpitters! You off early again?" he enquired.

"Not as early as we hoped. We wanted to get to the mine before there was anybody around. The trouble is that people might come investigating if they see us disappearing into the hill," explained Peter.

The vicar laughed and became serious. "There's

one thing that's been worrying my wife and me. We feel happy enough about your exploring this mine, although of course it's not our place to have any say in the matter; but what concerns us is the fact that we don't know where you are going. I mean, you might get lost or have an accident and no one would be able to find you. I know you want to keep it secret but in the interests of safety we should know where this mine is."

He paused to see how Peter would react. Peter thought for a moment. This was certainly a situation he had not foreseen. How silly of him; obviously someone ought to know. Ah well, he'd have to tell.

Before he could answer, Tim came to the rescue.

"I know what we'll do," he said. "We'll write down where the mine is and leave it with you. Then if we don't return by, say, seven o'clock, you can look at it. But you'll have to promise not to look at it before then."

The vicar laughed. "All right," he said, "I promise. Seriously though, that's a good idea. I won't stay now as I can see you're waiting to get off. What time do you expect to be back?"

"It's hard to say," said Peter, and then he explained: "If the mine is only short, we will probably go over to Eyam. Tim's been pestering me to go to a cave there. We went last year but didn't have much time to spend in it. He seems to have liked it and hasn't stopped talking about it since. If the mine's really long, and we hope it is, we won't be back till teatime. In any case, we'll be back before seven—all being well, of course!"

Peter made a rough drawing of the site of the mine, folded it up and handed it to the vicar. They walked to the vicarage gates together, where they said good-bye. Although it was still fairly early, the air was getting hot and it looked as though they were in for a sweltering day. The flies and midges pestered them as they walked to the mine, nearly driving them mad. The air was still, very still, even when they reached the top of the valley. They felt really excited. Once outside the mine, they changed quickly.

Warm underclothing, the long, woolly kind, covered by a one-piece boiler suit was their main clothing, with nailed climbing boots on their feet. As well as the long ladder and rope, they both carried a few feet of thin nylon rope wound round their waists. For lights they had acetylene lamps fitting onto lightweight helmets, and, as an emergency, candles. These went in their pockets, with matches, in a plastic waterproof bottle.

The lamps were made with two chambers, one for water and the other for carbide. The water dripped slowly onto the carbide, making acetylene gas which was piped to a jet in a reflector in the front of the lamp, where it was lit. These lamps would burn for nearly four hours on one filling, but they were bringing spare carbide as they were not sure how long the trip would take.

They also had a camera. This was a very old one that Peter had brought in case anything went wrong with the good one. Now they were very glad they had brought it with them to Hasslow. To take a photograph underground, they opened the shutter for a time exposure and lit a length of magnesium ribbon, which burnt for a few seconds with an intense bright light. Two or three inches of ribbon at f.11 with fast film.

As soon as they had put their stuff inside the entrance, they made ready for the battle ahead. Their lamps lit with a pop, and, once the flames had steadied themselves, the boys peered into the gloom. After the warmth of the outside air, the mine was freezing cold, and they tried not to touch the rocks which felt like lumps of ice. There seemed to be more draught blowing out than there had been the day before, and they shivered in spite of their warm clothing.

Squeezing through the boulder block at the entrance, they hurried on along the narrow passage by which they had gone the day before. When they got to the point where the passage divided, they went a short way down the left-hand one and paused to adjust their lamps. They soon turned back; it was not very inviting and they were keen to see what lay across the bridge. They were surprised how far it was. They thought it had been a lot closer to the entrance.

Here they uncoiled the rope, Tim tied one end round himself, and Peter held the other end in the way they had learnt at school. As Tim walked slowly across the bridge, Peter paid out the rope. When it came to Peter's turn to make the crossing, the same method was used; this time the rope was taken in by Tim. As he made his way across, Peter paused to peer down into the black pit. The sides were sheer, and right below was a still sheet of murky water. He kicked down a piece of mud from his boots and the water broke into a series of ripples. "Just like black ink," he thought.

"Come on; hurry up," called Tim, who was getting rather worried in case the bridge collapsed. "If you fall in, I'm jolly well not going to be able to hold on for ever."

To fall in; what a ghastly thought! Peter's stomach turned at it. To be standing on the edge and then to fall in and find there was no way out, only smooth, slippery walls—Ugh! And yet, when he got to the other side, he saw a sight that really made him go cold. On the very edge of the mud were the prints of fingers and, leading up to them, footmarks, facing the wall as though someone lost without a light had been groping along the wall. As though someone was lost. . . . Peter and Tim stared at the marks with growing horror. Their first reaction was to bolt for the entrance and open air. Turning slowly to Tim, Peter said,

"You remember the man that the vicar told us about, who came in here alone? Well, I reckon that's where he went. How horrible! Let's move on quickly. I don't think this mine has a friendly feeling about it at all. It's completely different from a cave."

They moved on, and rounding a bend came to a point where another passage ran across the one they were in, and the rails turned down the left-hand passage. Their passage went straight on as before but without any rails.

"It looks as though we've come to a main dividing of the ways," said Peter as they stopped. "I'm in favour of going straight on, as we want to explore the whole mine. What do you think?"

"I shouldn't think it goes far ahead," observed Tim, "or they'd have put rails in it. It does seem like a main passage, though. Perhaps they had rails down at one time but took them up when there was no lead left to work."

In one place part of the roof was held up by wood which was rotten, and they hurried by it. The limestone, which had been so solid before, was filled with large cracks, and in the passage were lumps of stone. Tim slowed down.

"I should think this is a patch of rock that's unsafe. Probably in a minute we'll come to a bit that's timbered up completely."

He was right about the roof needing support, for almost at once they came to a stretch, not timbered but built up with stone in the shape of an arch.

"It'll be safe enough," said Peter, noticing Tim was hanging back a bit. "The stones will be solid as long as we don't touch them or pull them out. Don't let's talk too loudly, though."

This unsafe part lasted only a few yards, and they came again into the ordinary passage, although it appeared a bit smaller.

Another fifty feet and they came out into a smallish chamber. They looked around. The roof was not very high and was streaked with white veins.

Small stalactites were hanging from it, showing the boys that this part was natural. This was the first natural part of the mine they had come to, and it was a welcome relief after all the artificial passages they had travelled along. There is something deeply satisfying about a natural cave to a caver; it is far more friendly than a mine.

The floor was strewn with large rocks cemented to the ground with hardened mud. At the far end, on the top of a ledge, the way seemed to go on. When they followed it, it became too narrow and they had to retreat. The passage grew smaller and smaller until it closed down completely.

Back in the chamber once again, they took a photograph and retraced their steps, relieved when they had got safely past the built-up parts. Once again a decision had to be made at the crossroads. In spite of the inviting looks the rails gave, they chose the other passage, deciding to leave what seemed the best till last. They had plenty of time. The passage was very narrow and low. It twisted a lot, and they decided it must have followed a vein of lead. While discussing this, they came out into another chamber, larger than the other but with the same kind of low roof.

In comparison with the other, the floor was very smooth, although not flat, and almost clear of rock. Down the walls were curious brown pipe effects caused by water deposits of thousands of years. This brown covering was spread over the floor as though a giant had been icing a cake with a slushy brown icing that had suddenly set. The boys hit their heads on the roof once or twice, although with their helmets on they felt only a jar. Once again the way appeared to continue straight on, but it closed down fairly soon. This disappointed them but, making sure there was definitely no way on, they returned to the crossroads once again.

"Well," announced Peter dramatically, "here we go: two intrepid explorers."

Their lamps lit up the rails well and showed the way ahead clearly. They started to trot slowly, impatient to see what was in store for them. Tim was some way ahead and Peter called to him to wait.

"Hang on," he said. "If you look at the roof you'll see it hasn't been mined. There are small stalactites on it."

They stopped and inspected. Tim, who was looking at the walls, gave a shout.

"The *walls* are mined; you can see the drill marks in them."

Sure enough, at intervals along the walls, were marks as though a candle had been pressed sideways into them when they were soft and then removed, leaving an impression.

"It looks as though we might be onto something at last," exclaimed Peter. "This is obviously a natural passage that's been enlarged by mining, so there might be a cavern in a minute. I hope so; this mine seems odd and it's getting me down. That's probably only because of all the stories the vicar's been telling us, but even so I shan't be sorry when we're finished in here!"

They pressed on until they came to another chamber, bigger than any they had been in before. The roof was a lot higher, and Peter reckoned it must have been about forty feet wide and about twenty high. The way on seemed clear enough and Tim went ahead. There was a loud splash and Peter looked to see his friend knee deep in water. Tim soon made his way back and explained what had happened. He was standing on the top of a rock, not realising that there was water in front of him. Peter could not see how it was possible to step into a pool of deep water without seeing it, until he did exactly the same. The water was absolutely clear and, when lit only from the front, was invisible. They found quite a few pools in that chamber, but the one Tim had found first of all presented an obstacle as it completely barred the way on.

"Ah well," sighed Peter, "there's nothing to it but to wade. It's not the first time we've had to get wet in a cave."

They moved all perishable articles into higher pockets and stepped in. At once the water filled their boots and gave a pleasant sensation as it crept round the toes. The water pressed their overalls tight against their legs but, once the initial shock of the cold water was over, they hardly noticed it.

Going was slow, as mud was stirred up from the bottom as they walked, hiding the rock in a thick fog. After a bit the water got deeper, and when it reached their waists they wondered if they ought to go on.

"I think we should stop and go back," said Peter.

"Oh, let's go on a bit further," pleaded Tim, although his teeth were chattering. The ceiling was low and they could not see far ahead.

Peter relented because he also wanted to see what was beyond. "Okay," he said, "but don't start grumbling if you have wet sandwiches for lunch. They aren't usually very appetising that way."

As he finished speaking, Tim disappeared from view and then rose up spluttering and gurgling. His helmet was still on but his light was out. He struggled back to Peter, spitting out water by the pint.

"Well," enquired Peter, "do you still want to go on?"

Tim emptied out his ears and then grinned. "We must be standing on a sort of ledge because I just stepped off into space, only it wasn't space but water. It must be jolly deep because I didn't touch the bottom. You and your wretched mine; give me my cave at Eyam any time! I don't suppose we can get across the water now."

"Not today, anyway. Perhaps we could have another go tomorrow, with a raft, if we can get something small enough to bring down. At the moment I can't think of anything. I don't fancy swimming it with all our clothes on, and it's too cold to start undressing. Let's go back and see what else there is in that chamber. I'll light your lamp with mine."

The chamber they had just left had massive

boulders on the floor, but a path had been cleared
for the rails which led into the water. It was partly
because of the rails going into the water that the
boys had been so keen to pass it. They searched for
some time for another way out but had to admit
defeat. On the right-hand side a rift ran up
some way into the roof, but it looked too hard to
climb.

Suddenly Peter let out a whoop. "Just see how
dense we've been. The clue to the way out has
been staring us in the face the whole time and we
haven't even noticed it." He pointed to the ground
under the rift and said, "What's that?"

Tim glanced and said, "Why, just a spare length
of rail. Hardly a clue to the way out."

"Truck rail be jiggered!" shouted Peter. "Take
another look and then guess again."

Tim came over to where Peter was standing. "I
say!" he exclaimed. "It's an old iron ladder." He
looked up into the rift. "It must have fallen from
up there so . . ."

"That's the way on," finished Peter. "Now all
we have to do is to find a way up. I imagine the
ladder will go up a good way so let's stand that up."

Standing the ladder up proved to be a very difficult job as it was extremely heavy and unwieldy.
At last it was up reasonably secure and Peter
climbed first. At the top, a small hole led into an
equally small passage, and he pulled himself into
the hole by gripping a miniature stalagmite pillar
sprouting from the floor about three feet in. The
floor was smooth and he slid in quite easily. Once

in, he went on until he could turn round, and then he returned on his stomach. Tim wondered what had happened to Peter and was relieved to see a light reappear far above him. Peter called to him to come up, and they were soon together again.

Peter had to back to let Tim in, and he passed him one end of the rope round his waist and told him to tie it onto the ladder.

"We can't risk its falling away and leaving us," he explained.

With Peter leading they squirmed their way through the passage, which was arrayed with small pillars like the one Peter had used to pull himself in. They found these very useful for pulling themselves along. Twisting about, the passage was climbing steadily, although still only high enough to lie down in.

"Isn't the floor smooth?" remarked Tim, fascinated by the ease with which they slid.

"Yes, I shouldn't think we're the first to come this way. Probably all the old miners used it, although I can't think how they got their stuff back, but I suppose they did somehow. We'll probably find out when we get to the top, which shouldn't be . . . Hey!"

As he spoke, his voice suddenly sounded flat and faint and everything seemed dark. Looking up, there appeared to be no roof, and for a moment Peter thought they had come out into the night until he realised it was still day-time. They scrambled out of the hole and looked around.

They had come out into a massive dripping chamber whose roof and walls they could hardly see with their acetylene lamps. They gasped for breath. They had seen some largish chambers in other parts of the country, but not as large as this —and in Derbyshire. . . . Well!

Chapter 11

A RIDE

For a long time they gazed around the chamber, enthralled by its size. They had entered near one end, for behind them a wall was clearly visible, rising up to be lost in the gloom. It was Peter who broke the spell.

"Crumbs!" was all he could say, but it was sufficient to bring them down to earth.

"I've got a bit of magnesium ribbon," he added after a bit. "I'll light a length."

He unrolled a few inches, snapped it off and hung it from the end of a piece of stick. He held the end in the flame of his lamp. It glowed, sparkled and immediately flared into life. The powerful light it gave penetrated the farthest corners of the chamber and they could see clearly all about them. High up in the roof hung a slender, solitary stalactite over twenty feet long. Curious formations covered the walls. The left-hand wall was nearly upright, with the right wall sloping towards it. The floor was also slanting, away from the left-hand wall, making a triangle.

The flare spluttered and went out. In the darkness that followed they imagined they could still see about them, so bright had the light been.

"How big do you reckon it is?" gasped Tim, referring to the chamber.

"Well, it's bigger than anything we've seen, isn't it? I should say it's well over a hundred feet high and probably somewhere near three hundred feet long. At its widest, what, about two hundred feet? That's monstrous for a Derbyshire cave. We've certainly made a discovery here. I wonder if it leads anywhere."

"Well," said Tim, jumping onto a higher rock, "let's find out."

"Wait a sec," pleaded Peter. "Let's have some chocolate; I feel famished. You've got it, I think."

Tim fished in his pockets. "Yep," he said. "It's a bit wet, I'm afraid," he continued, pulling out a soggy mass. "I think it's only the paper that's affected, though."

They munched chocolate as silently as chocolate can be munched, and then they moved off. The floor was strewn with large boulders, and as they picked their way amongst them they felt like insects crawling in a coal cellar.

Just over half way along, they came to a part where a deep gulley was cut into the rock floor.

"It's a canyon," explained Peter.

The explanation did not seem to do much good.

"A what?" asked Tim.

"A canyon. You know, a place where a river cuts itself into the ground. If we look round, I expect we'll see a . . . ah yes, over there." He pointed to a passage coming in on the left. "The water probably flowed out of there and cut this. It won't be very important, so we'll have a look at it on the way back. It probably leads back to a choked surface feed on the moor."

The canyon was only a few feet deep and they clambered down easily.

"Look, more rails," cried Peter. "And trucks this time. That's odd. We didn't see any trucks down below. I wonder what happened to them."

They inspected one of the trucks which was built of wood. The part that held the minerals was 'V' shaped and strengthened by iron struts. The wood was wet and rather rotten. When Peter squeezed one of the planks it was rather like squeezing a sponge.

Two trucks were chained to the side, and as Peter looked at them a thought came to him.

"I wonder," he mused, looking at the wheels, "I wonder if they'd still run."

They unchained the first one and rocked it backwards and forwards on the rails. At first nothing happened, and then with a snap the wheels started to turn. They pushed the truck forwards and soon it was running reasonably smoothly.

"Do you think we could . . . go for a trip in it?" whispered Tim, really excited at the idea.

Peter thought for a moment. "I'm keen to," he said. "The rails run slightly downhill so there'll be no trouble there. I can't see what harm we can come to as long as we've got lights. After all, they couldn't go very fast on this slope. Let's make sure the sides aren't going to collapse; I don't want to be ejected half way down. You get in and I'll push off."

Tim climbed in then Peter positioned himself behind, ready to push.

"Okay?" he called out.

"Okay driver, take her away."

Peter heaved and the truck moved slowly away. As soon as it had gathered enough speed to keep going by itself, Peter jumped on board. The truck swayed and Tim shouted in alarm. After a moment it settled down and they both peered in front ready to enjoy the journey.

"Yahoo, ride him, cowboy!" shouted Tim, beating the sides of the truck.

Clankerty clank, clankerty clank. The sound made by the wheels running over the rails was increasing in speed now and they could feel a wind in their faces. Suddenly the passage got narrower and steeper and they could have touched both sides easily.

"I should keep your hands in," warned Peter as the track took a sudden turn to the right, making the truck lean and threaten to overturn.

Suddenly a horrible thought struck Tim.

"I say, supposing we want to get out: what do we do?"

Peter did not answer. He had already thought of that. Instead of replying, he tried to be cheerful and remarked.

"It's quite thrilling, isn't it? Almost like being on a ghost train."

A ghost train? Almost as soon as he spoke, he

H

realised he had said the wrong thing. What a peculiar noise! Something hissing like an angry snake. Pssssssss!

He turned round to see what it was and the sound stopped. No, there it was from the front. He turned back again. Now there were two. Psssss pfft! Everything went a few shades darker.

"What's happened?" he called out.

Tim sounded worried. "My lamp's blown out."

"Your lamp's blown out? Heavens!"

Psssss pfft! Blackness.

"Mine has, too," said Peter dryly.

Clankerty clank, clankerty clank. The sounds were coming so quickly now that it was almost impossible to separate them. They were going really fast by this time and Peter was hunting frantically in his pocket for his torch. Just as he was about to give up, he found it. Quickly he shone it down the track.

"Look out! Duck!" he cried.

A low beam was looming up ahead. Although Tim ducked, Peter was not so lucky. The beam hit his helmet with a crack and sent it flying from his head. He felt a terrific jar and saw stars for a moment. Although dazed, he recovered at once, to become aware of their perilous position.

In the light of his torch they could see that they had reached another chamber. Standing half way along the track was another truck and Tim gave a warning shout.

"Brace yourself!" he shouted.

Crash! They hit with an impact that all but

threw them from the truck. The torch flew out of Peter's hand, but before the echo of the crash had died away they both leapt from their truck, which was starting to move again. They stood in the blackness in silence, thinking over their nightmare ride. The silence was almost immediately shattered by a deep, booming, clanking sound, as though it were raining scrap iron and drums. The sound had not properly faded away before it was followed by a similar sound, making them jump in fright again.

They could light their lamps by means of a flint fixed to the reflector, and Tim re-lit his with a pop. To their amazement, both trucks had disappeared. The rails rounded a large boulder and they walked round it to see what had caused all the noise. There the rails ended suddenly at the edge . . . at the edge of a shaft. Peter looked at the open mouth and felt quite dizzy. Quietly he lay down. Everything was rather hazy. He was vaguely conscious of Tim flopping down next to him. He thought of saying something about what a lucky escape they had had, but he thought better of it. Such a statement would only be pointing out the obvious and would not help matters in any way. Instead, he said nothing and they rested in silence for a time.

The dizzy feeling had passed, and slowly Peter got to his feet. His legs were trembling a little, but he made his way by the light of his torch to the edge of the shaft and threw a stone down. It boomed to the bottom in much the same way as the trucks.

"How are you feeling, Tim?" asked Peter. "Do you feel okay for a ladder descent?"

Tim got to his feet. "Yes, I'm okay. I just sort of felt a bit funny when I saw what had nearly happened to us. How far down do you reckon it goes?"

"I don't know. I should think the best part of a hundred feet, so we'll need all our ladder. You join it together and tether it, and I'll nip back and get my helmet and lamp. It shouldn't be far back."

Peter disappeared into the darkness, leaving Tim to see to the ladder. Tim joined the four lengths together, tethered one end to a strong section of the rails and tossed the other end down the shaft. It slithered down easily and pulled taut with a twang. He uncoiled the life-line and laid it out on the floor above the shaft. There was no sign of Peter returning, so he started to look around the chamber. It was definitely smaller than the one they had just come from, but it was still impressive. The walls were bare of formations and the place had a rugged look about it.

Feeling rather cold after his ducking, he decided to go along the passage that continued out of the chamber. Here again the rails started, and he had visions of finding chamber after chamber as he remembered some cavers did in the Pyrenees. There, the chambers could have held cathedrals. But while these were much smaller, they were, well, they were their own which made them better. Thinking on these lines, he suddenly came across a pile of boulders blocking the way. These ran right up to the roof and there was no way beyond.

He shone his light around and was amazed to see that the walls were covered with a sort of silvery sheen, and the veins of dark, lumpy metal ran thickly everywhere. Then he caught sight of something that made him jump. In one place by the fall of rock was a curious mark on the wall like a claw

Like a claw? His blood ran cold. This was one of the Dragon's claw marks that the mine had been named after. Supposing it was *the* mark. How grotesque it looked. He shuddered and went back to see if Peter had arrived. He found him peering down the shaft, wondering if his friend had gone down on his own.

"I hope you didn't get fed up waiting," said Peter, "but the passage divided some way back and I took the wrong turning."

"Never mind that," said Tim. "I've got something to show you. Bring the camera."

They set off down the tunnel and soon came to the roof fall.

"There!" said Tim dramatically.

"Crumbs! Then this must be the place where they were working when the place blew up. We must certainly have a photograph of that. Doesn't it look horrible!"

They propped up the camera and lit the magnesium ribbon. In the bright light, the claw, which was about eighteen inches across, looked even worse as coloured streaks in the rock looked like veins running along it.

"I don't know much about mining," admitted Peter, "but I should reckon that this is a very rich vein of lead. It seems to lead under that fall of rock. It would be pretty hard to clear. It would be worth it, though. You can almost pull this stuff away in your hands, there's so much of it. No wonder the owners didn't want to stop working it. Come on; let's get back. This claw gives me the creeps!"

They hurried back to the ladder and rope and drew lots for who was to go down first. Their method of choosing was quite simple. One of them would hold a small stone in one hand and nothing in the other. If the other person picked the hand with the stone, he went first. Peter won and made ready for the descent. He tied the life-line round his waist and Tim tied himself to the rails with the short length of rope he carried. When all was ready, Peter stepped into the shaft and bade his friend farewell.

"Hang on," said Tim. "I'll take a photograph of you. Blow your lamp out."

Once again they set the camera up and the ribbon flared. When the shutter was closed, Peter lit his lamp and started off.

As he climbed slowly down, he could feel the ladder swinging about below and he wondered if it would be long enough. He need not have worried, for about two-thirds of the way down he came to a wooden platform, part of which had been broken by the falling trucks. On the platform were old picks and shovels, with their handles covered in a white creeper growth. Although they were rotten and rusty, they had an unabandoned look about them, as though they had been left just for the lunch hour.

The shaft continued on down for a short distance but was a dead end. Peter shouted up to let Tim know he was returning. When he felt the lifeline round his waist tighten, he started off. As he climbed he noticed his lamp was burning unsteadily. "Time to refill it," he thought.

Tim did not feel particularly keen to go down when he heard it was a dead end.

"Give me my cave at Eyam any time," he said.

"You and your wretched cave," laughed Peter. "Still, if you're a really good boy I'll take you there sometime before we go home. But you'll have to promise to behave!"

They refilled their lamps, took a photograph of the chamber and set back. They found a part where the tunnel and rails divided.

"That's where I went wrong," said Peter. "It doesn't go very far, though. It ended in a blank wall."

Returning to the large chamber, they were amazed again by the size of it.

"Well," said Peter, "now we've seen the lot. Except for that small passage near the entrance. We can look in that on the way back, but I shouldn't think it goes very far. I'm in favour of a spot of lunch just now."

As Tim pulled the bag from his pocket, one corner of it collapsed and water gushed out.

"Mmmm," said Peter. "Bread and water sandwiches, I see. Delicious!"

Tim shook the bag violently, spraying Peter. "You should be thankful we've got anything to eat at all, with your encouraging me to take swimming lessons at odd times."

Peter put one in his mouth. "Sorry about my rude remarks. I take it all back. These sandwiches are simply lovely. They're still warm, in fact."

Peter reflected on this statement for a moment and then shouted, *"Still warm!* Hey, where have you been keeping these?"

Tim laughed as he explained. "Well, you see, I wanted to keep them as dry as possible so I put them in my top inside pocket. But, I suppose it isn't very nice to have body-warm sandwiches."

Peter just shuddered and ate in silence.

As soon as they had finished, they made their way back to the bridge without mishap. This they crossed quickly, avoiding looking at the fingerprints on the pit edge. The sooner they were passed the better! If the boys got lost now, they definitely would not be the first.

Chapter 12

OLD WORKINGS

"What an ass I am!" exclaimed Peter.

"Congratulations."

Peter and Tim stood in silence, after these two remarks, at the small passage near the entrance. As Peter did not explain his somewhat startling confession, Tim prompted him further.

"What is it," he asked, "that's suddenly made you realise your grade of intelligence?"

"You know at the entrance there was quite a breeze blowing out?"

"Yes."

"Well, did you notice it once we were inside?"

"No, I didn't. But what's so brilliant about that?"

Peter said nothing but led Tim into the small passage they had not yet bothered about. Here a breeze was blowing quite hard. Tim realised the significance of this at once and started off down the passage.

"Well," he said, "this means that this passage leads a long way. I wonder what lies down here."

Thrilled, they hurried along the passage which in many ways was similar to the smaller ones they had explored in other parts of the mine. But their excitement was short-lived for they emerged into a small chamber which appeared to be the end. They paused to look about them to see if there was a hidden way on. The breeze had gone, much to their amazement, and they could see there was definitely no way out.

"I think we ought to call this Disappointment Chamber," grumbled Tim. "I was sure we were going to find something big."

They took another photograph, although the place was not particularly attractive, and with heavy hearts made their way back. The day was finished.

In the passage Peter stopped suddenly. "Am I going mad or something?" he said. "Can you feel a draught now?"

Tim said, "Yes," and they decided to go back towards the chamber to see where it stopped. There seemed to be no sudden stop, but they just realised it was not there.

"This is daft," said Peter. "A draught has got to come from somewhere. It can't just start for no reason at all, in the middle of a passage."

Tim was the first to discover the answer to the riddle. In the roof of the passage was a hole going upwards. They shone their lights up and it seemed to go vertically for some way.

"The problem is," said Peter, "how are we going to climb? The sides are almost sheer . . . no . . . there are sort of grooves cut in the side. I suppose they're meant for climbing."

They picked for who was to go first, and Tim won.

"I'll take some ladder with me," he said. "Then it will be easier for one of us on the way down."

Peter helped Tim haul himself into the hole and watched him start to climb. Small stones falling at intervals told Peter that his friend was still climbing, and he was amazed by the height of the shaft.

"Can you see the top yet?" he called up.

"Yes, I think I'm coming to it now." Tim's voice was very faint. "Yes, I'm at the top." Then after a pause: "Ladder coming down."

There was a clatter and a twang and Peter saw that the ladder had not been quite long enough to reach the passage. By starting to climb the shaft as Tim had done, Peter soon got onto the ladder. On the way up he was surprised to see the ladder had been joined by links.

"That means the shaft is over twenty-five feet," he thought.

As he reached the top he was greeted by Tim, who said, "I hope you didn't get smothered in ladder, but I threw down fifty feet in case the shaft was more than twenty-five."

Peter laughed. "Don't go grey when I tell you that fifty feet was too short!"

"*Too short!* Great Scott. To think I climbed all that without even a safety line!"

"I shouldn't worry if I were you. The shaft was too narrow to fall far. I nearly got jammed once or twice. All the same, we mustn't forget that this sort of thing can be dangerous. Now, what have you found up here?"

"There's a passage that goes along some way. I only looked along it as there wasn't time to explore. You arrived too jolly quickly. That seems about all. One hopeful thing is that the draught is still with us. Let's hope it keeps that way."

Peter emerged from the shaft completely and turned so that the light from his helmet swung round the walls and shone down the passage.

"Are you content now," asked Peter, "or do you still want to go to *your* cave?"

"Oh, this will do for now," said Tim, and then he added: "As long as we visit it before we go home."

"Okay. This looks older than the other parts of the mine," observed Peter, as they were making their way along the low and twisting passage. "I can't see any drill marks. Look!"

He stopped and picked up a wooden object which fell to pieces in his hands.

"Tim," he said, "that was an old clog. It must have been *jolly* old. Fancy finding one here."

It was not long before Tim found another. They examined this one on the ground. It was just plain wood, black now and split badly in places. It was covered with the same white growth that had covered the tools found down the shaft in the main part of the mine. It was obviously worth a photograph.

Once they had found these things, they began to look out for more and were rewarded by one or two interesting finds. The roof had been blackened in places by the lights the old miners had carried, and on the walls various people had smoked their initials.

"I wish we could find a date," said Peter thoughtfully. "I reckon this part is jolly old. It's hard to tell, though. We might just have missed seeing the drill marks, but everything is so crude and uneven for . . . Look, here's an opening at last. It's good to be able to straighten up again after being bent double for so long. I thought my neck was going to break, it was aching so much."

Although only a small chamber, it was a very welcome relief, and the boys stood for some time just getting their limbs working. When they started to look around, Peter immediately gave a shout.

"Look at that," he said, pointing to a date smoked on the wall. "1665. This part must be old. Hang on; that date rings a bell. I can't place it for a moment. It came in History last term but I don't suppose it has any bearing on this mine."

The date was over a wall built up of stone, and one or two of the stones had been pulled away and were lying on the ground. Over the date a cross had been smoked but it did not seem to be of any significance. The boys peered inside and could see some tools lying around and some mouldy stuff that looked like clothing. The date 1665 was bothering Peter so much that he hardly heard Tim say he was going through the hole to investigate.

Just as Tim got inside, the light suddenly dawned upon Peter.

"Get out!" he almost screamed. "Get out!"

Tim was most alarmed and obeyed as quickly as possible, knocking his knees and elbows in the process.

"What on earth? I nearly wrecked my knees getting out. Look at them." He started to pull up the legs of his boiler suit.

"Do you realise that you've probably just escaped with your life and all you can do is to grumble about your wretched knees?"

"My life?" queried Tim.

"Yes, and your knees. Just as you got in I remembered about that date and realised why it was here with a cross over it. 1665 was the date of the Great Plague of London!"

"Well?" Tim could see no connection between himself and a plague in London three hundred years ago.

"You probably don't know, but the Plague also came this way to Eyam, which is pretty close. It got brought there in some old clothes or something. I guess some of the miners who worked here came from Eyam and were infected by the Plague and died down here. They were probably put in there and the place blocked up to stop the disease spreading. That's why there's a cross on the wall as well as the date. I don't know how long germs last; probably there would be no danger after all these years, but I thought it best to get you out of there as quickly as possible."

"Thanks," said Tim, who had broken out in a cold sweat. "I suppose the men were dead when they were blocked up. I mean, you never know what people will do when they're afraid. The other miners might have got scared and . . . Okay, I got a bit carried away. Come on; let's move. I'm sorry."

When they went into the continuing passage they saw that it had a very uneven and rocky floor. The length seemed endless, the boys expecting to come to the end at any moment. Once or twice they wondered if perhaps they ought to turn back but, deciding they had enough spare carbide and water to keep their lamps going quite a few hours, they continued, intrigued as to where they would end up. Surely the end would be open; the draught was still with them.

"Any idea where we're going?" asked Tim.

"Under the moor, away from the valley, I should think. We seem to have gone miles, though. I feel I'd give almost anything to be able to stand up straight for a while. I think I must be breaking in half. Let's lie down for a bit, to rest and stretch at the same time. There's no real hurry."

They rested for a short time on the cold, damp ground but they were too impatient to wait long. They went on and on, pressing their way into the heart of the limestone that made up the countryside around. Far, far above them the sun was probably shining and the birds singing, but the boys were in a land of perpetual night, broken for a fraction of eternity by two boys who depended for so much on their artificial lighting. To be without those lights would mean that the darkness could claim them for ever; whilst they had those lights

they were the conquerors. Peter took off his helmet
and looked at the steady flame of his lamp. All was
well.

Tim was leading and suddenly he stopped in his
tracks. Peter, following close behind, almost
bumped into him.

"Sssh," said Tim, drawing backwards slightly.

In the passage in front of him was a pile of
rock like a roof fall and in the pile was a gleaming
circle like an eye. Tim thought of the Greek legen-
dary weird sisters who lived in a cave and had one
eye which they passed around as needed. Perhaps
this was it, or even the Dragon!

Realising that this was hardly likely, although
the mine seemed capable of anything, he went forward to investigate.

Lying on the rock was a modern sixpence which
reflected the light from their helmets. A sixpence?
Hardly the thing to find down a mine that had
only just been opened. Tim saw an explanation.

"Someone must have come in here when we were
in the other part. He may still be ahead of us and
in a moment he'll come pouncing out. Woooh!"

"No, I think we're getting rather jumpy after all
the things that have happened to us today. I hardly
think that anyone could have come along here and
then dropped a sixpence. He'd have needed a good
light, and this is hardly the first passage anyone
would come along."

"I know, but look at the date of the thing. It's
been made only two years. Jolly queer, isn't it?"

Peter was thinking. "There's only one faint explanation," he said thoughtfully, "but it seems too fantastic. You remember the first day we came on the moor we looked down a shaft and you accidentally dropped a sixpence?"

"Yes."

"Well, we may be under the shaft now. All these stones may be stuff that's fallen or been thrown down it."

Carefully they climbed to the top, removed their lights from their helmets and looked up. Far away they could see a tiny patch of light.

"Crumbs!" exclaimed Tim. "Just think how far we've come. Well over a mile. That's terrific!"

"Even better now you've got your sixpence back," teased Peter.

They clambered over the boulders but the passage stopped almost at once.

"Well," said Peter, "this is Journey's End. Let's get back; I'm starting to feel cold."

Tim hesitated. "I don't suppose we could climb the shaft and get out that way."

"Blow me, it's two hundred feet. If you think I'm going to climb that without a life-line, you're very much mistaken. Besides, we don't know the condition of the shaft; it must be three or four hundred years old. I agree it looks as though it could be climbed. If you want to, you go ahead; I'm going back the long way. If you do try, I won't guarantee your future happiness, as our hold-up friend would put it. Come on, old son, this is the best way."

With this, he pulled Tim gently away from the

I

shaft up which he was still gazing wistfully.

"Besides," continued Peter, "you don't want anything to happen to you before you make a will leaving me your new-found wealth, do you?"

Although the way back seemed shorter than expected, they were feeling pretty exhausted and they flopped down on the hillside under a blazing sun. No one had been around to witness their sudden arrival into the world of light, and they dragged their kit outside and closed the boulder.

"The problem now," said Peter after some time, "is what to do with the mine. I suppose we'd better go to Mad Sam and tell him all about it. What's the time, by the way?"

Tim dived into the rucksack where he had put his watch for safety.

"It can't be!" he exclaimed when he looked at it. "Surely not. What time do you think it is, Peter?"

"Dunno. About two?"

"Well, it's jolly well half past five. We won't be able to see Mad Sam today. We'll have to go in the morning. Let's go down to the river and wash. I'm absolutely filthy. I can't put on my other clothes when I'm in this state."

They scrambled down to the river and peeled off their wet clothing. Peter jumped in and came up spluttering. Tim, just to be different, dived in. Although the river was not exactly deep, a shallow dive was possible without too much danger of a cracked skull. The bottom was soft mud and the worst to be expected was a stuck head. They washed the mud from the mine off their bodies, quickly rubbed themselves down with a towel and got dressed.

"Nice to have clean clothes," remarked Peter. "Come on; let's get back or Mr. Parkinson will be wondering where we are."

Their kit, soaked with water, seemed very heavy as they trudged their way back. They made frequent exchanges of the rucksack. As they reached the vicarage gates, the vicar came out to meet them.

"I hope you're not worried about us," said Peter, thinking they might be considered late.

"No, no, not at all. I came out to let you know there's some tea for you. We thought you'd be pretty tired, and it's quite a job having to cook a meal when you're worn out, so come along in when you've dumped your stuff. There are also a couple of parcels for the pair of you that a Mr. Wheeler brought in today."

The boys thanked him and, as they not only wanted to see the parcels but were starving, they wasted no time in getting back to the vicarage. The first parcel contained the two cameras that Mr. Wheeler has promised, together with some film and a letter of thanks from the company. The second parcel puzzled them, for they had not expected anything else. When they opened it, they found two books and a letter. Peter read it aloud.

Dear Timpitters,

I doubt if we will meet again on the Hasslow

Moor as we are not continuing with the search. We doubt now if we would ever find the mine.

When I mentioned your 'heroic' actions to the heads of the firm, they insisted on buying the cameras. This left me with nothing to give you, so I started to look for something else. I remembered all you had told me in the Land Rover coming back from the moor, about your caving interests, so I decided to give you each a book— one on the caves and mines of Derbyshire for Peter, as it is his home county, and a book of French caving adventures for Tim, as he seems to like adventure and did mention he wanted to explore a French cave.

I have also remembered what you told me when we first met. My son has certainly been a changed boy recently. There must be something to this Christianity. He could never have changed by himself! I'm going to the service with him this Sunday.

                    Yours truly,
                    David Wheeler.

"Well, that's terrific!" exclaimed Peter. "All because of a chance meeting."

"Chance?" Tim raised his eyebrows.

Peter grinned. "I didn't mean to say that. I meant an unexpected meeting. God gives us opportunities we don't expect."

"I should think Mr. Wheeler expected it less than we did! I do hope he really wants to become a Christian. We must carry on praying for him.

Now, is that book good?"

"Yes, it's one I've been wanting for ages, but it was too expensive. It's quite scarce now, I believe, as it's been out of print for some time. This is wonderful."

Tim was equally delighted with his book as he had read quite widely on the French caves such as the Haut Garonne, Pierre Saint Martin and the Henne Mort. As he had told Mr. Wheeler, one of his ambitions was to go to France.

"Is there anything about Dragon's Claw Mine in your book?" asked Tim.

"I'll see." Peter thumbed through the index. "No, I didn't think there would be. After all, no one really knows much about it."

"Well, you'll have to send the publishers a report so they can add it to the next edition if they print one." Tim was half joking.

"Yes. Seriously, though, I suppose we'll have to tell someone. It's a bit mean keeping a mine and cave as large as that a secret. That large chamber must be one of the biggest in Derbyshire. I'd sort of imagined the mine was ours and our secret. It's going to be rotten to have to share it, in a way. Of course," he continued, brightening up, "it all depends on what Mad Sam says. If he tells us to keep quiet about where it is, we'll have to. Let's wait and see what he says before we get too worked up. In a way, I hope he tells us to keep it a secret."

Tim felt the same way about the mine. Certainly it was a bit mean to keep a discovery quiet, but when you've found it, well, things seem a bit different somehow. They felt they were fortunate to have someone else to make the decision for them.

Peter looked at the book again. "It does mention *your* cave." Peter enjoyed teasing his friend.

"My cave? Quick; let me see."

Peter held the book out of his reach. "Now, now," he said; "manners, please. Ask nicely."

Tim made another grab at the book but Peter still held it away.

The vicar, who had been standing watching for some time, now stepped up to prevent a fight.

"So you're the two heroes, are you?" he said. "I had an idea it might be you. Have you seen the papers?"

"No. Why?"

The vicar opened the local paper for the boys to see. On one page was quite a large report of the hold-up in which Peter and Tim, who went unnamed, featured quite prominently.

"Well, well," laughed the vicar, "the unknown heroes. Now tell me about your exploits in the mine today. Was it up to your expectations?"

"I'll say it was," said Peter. "Much better than we'd ever hoped. It's all ours now that the mining company has gone."

Then, with the help of Tim, he proceeded to tell the vicar all about their adventures, toning them down in places so that they seemed less dangerous. Mr. Parkinson, however, smiled at times as though he guessed the truth.

"What was this about your first meeting with Mr. Wheeler?" he asked. "It seems to me that you

had a good opportunity to tell him about what
God has done for you."

They told him what had happened.

"Well," the vicar continued, "don't forget what
people see you do as Christians counts as much as
what you say. You seem to have managed both
parts well this time."

"But this was exciting," said Peter. "It's not always so easy when it's not exciting!"

Chapter 13

THE SECRET

Walking up to Mad Sam's house the next morning, the two boys were feeling really thrilled about their find—also rather nervous about this visit. They had been guessing what Mad Sam's reactions would be when they told him about the mine. Peter thought he would thank them both, but Tim imagined his going into a rage at the idea of the mine having been found.

Still wondering, they approached the door and knocked hard. As they did so, their stomachs sank as they remembered their last visit. They waited for a shuffle in the house, but nothing happened.

Peter knocked again.

"Perhaps he's out," Tim suggested.

"I should hardly think so. He's nowhere to go unless he's toddled off to the village for his pension."

They waited but still no one came. Suddenly a thought struck Tim.

"You don't suppose he's ill, do you, Peter?"

"Could be, I suppose. Perhaps we'd better go in and see. I hope he isn't waiting for us with a gun or anything."

Somewhat hesitatingly, the boys opened the door and went in. On the table were the remains of a meal which looked as though they had been there a day or so. Peter smelt the milk.

"Pooh! Sour. I expect he *is* ill. His bed's next door, isn't it?"

Tim nodded and they stood and looked at each other. Neither wanted to go in for fear of what he might find. Eventually a sense of duty inspired Peter to push the door open. His heart leapt when he saw Mad Sam lying still in his bed.

At first Peter thought he was dead, but then he could hear very laboured breathing. The old man stirred as Peter went up to him, and his eyes flickered open.

"Who is it?" he croaked.

"It's the two boys who came here the other day to shelter from the storm," replied Peter. "Are you ill?"

The old man ignored this question, and his eyes lit up. "Did you find the mine?" he wheezed.

"I think you need a doctor," said Peter.

"No, no; a doctor'll do no good now. Never trust them, anyway. You haven't answered me. Did you find the mine?"

Peter had no idea what to do. Here was someone obviously seriously ill, and all he wanted to do was to talk about the mine. Peter made a decision.

"We're going for a doctor. We'll tell you about the mine later."

Mad Sam got worked up. "Tell me now, tell me now. There won't be a later. My life's nearly finished now."

With this, he started to get out of bed. Peter

changed his mind. He would tell him about the
mine and send Tim for a doctor.

"You'll do no such thing. If either of you tries
to go I'll get up and stop you."

Peter realised this would be fatal for an old man
in this state, so they sat down by the side of the bed
with every intention of making things as short as
possible. Both he and Tim were silently praying
that Mad Sam would recover.

"Right," said Peter, "we'll tell you about it."

And briefly they told him of the site, how long
the mine was and about the finding of the old
workings where they found the Plague burial
tomb.

Peter got up but Mad Sam told him to sit down.

"It's about mine. It's . . ." He started to cough
violently. "It's . . . ooof . . . important. Listen,
will yer. It can't wait 'cos I may be dead when you
returns. My old grandad worked there when he
was a young 'un and he found this old part just like
you did. He never told anyone but me. I remember
him telling me when I was a child."

Peter and Tim found it hard to imagine Mad
Sam as a child. The old man paused and then
continued.

"That left hand passage near the entrance was
never used, and one day he set about exploring and
found all them old passages. He broke into the
place with the date, not realising what it was. Inside he found a lot of skeletons and their tools. He
reckoned they were miners from Eyam. You did
well to guess they were connected with the Plague.

All those miners, and others killed in the mine, are what he called the Keepers of the Mine. They preserve the secret of the mine. But that's as may be. What I really wanted to tell you about was this terrible mystery, or secret, which means it must never be worked. You've not told anyone where it is, have you?"

"No," replied Peter; "no one knows but us."

Mad Sam paused for some time in deep thought. Probably he was trying to get some more strength. Eventually he looked up.

"I don't know how much you know about this mine but you've probably heard stories. Well, I can tell yer this. Get them out of your heads at once. They're false. False the lot of them. When the miners walked out and said the mine was haunted, they saved the village. Aye, I know it sounds kind of funny, but they knew the mine wasn't haunted."

"You mean they just said it so they couldn't work?" Peter was completely muddled. In his mind he wondered if Mad Sam knew what he was talking about.

"They did it because . . . Well, I'd better start at the beginning. The mining company were a hard lot of men and they used to treat the miners like slaves, aye, and like animals. The miners had to put up with the conditions as there was no other work. Now, they pushed on past an enormous chamber and came across a very rich vein of lead. Very soon they came to water which threatened to flood the whole mine. But that company, not car-

ing twopence about them miners' lives, made them
press on. Then a survey was made. That shook
them. That survey showed there was a terrible
lot of water under that part of the moor. So
much that if it broke out it would have flooded the
mine and rushed down the valley to swamp the
village. They were hard times and the employers
were hard people, too. That company couldn't care
if this happened or not, they were so greedy to get
the lead. Their homes weren't in the village so
what they said was: 'If we break through to the
water then we lose the lead, but if we don't work
it then we lose the lead in any case. So we might as
well try.'

"They kept the secret about the water from
the men so they wouldn't stop working. Even then,
there was a fair amount of water running, but a
level had been driven to take the water away. But
each day the water in the workings got more
until they started to flood. Each charge threatened
to break into the main reservoir, and the poor
men worked on without knowing a thing about
it.

"Just in time, my grandad got wind of it and
called a secret meeting. You see, we've been far-
mers round here for some time and, as our family
owned quite a bit of land, my grandad was a sort
of head workman. After the meeting, the miners
decided to leave the mine, and so as not to scare the
poor villagers they said the mine was haunted. Of
course, it wasn't. It was only as an excuse for leaving it.

"It meant leaving good work for a life of poverty. It was a great sacrifice, aye, a great sacrifice. One night my grandad secretly led a party down the mine and sealed up the workings completely. This was a hard job and one or two men nearly lost their lives. They worked all night in shifts and had it done before the owners got wise to it.

"The owners were raging when they did find out, and they did all they could to get them workers back. But did they manage? Aye, one or two did, but not many. Those that did weren't from this village, and they were soon set on by the Hasslow men. Of course, this state of affairs couldn't go on for ever, and the owners said they would do another survey. If the water was found to be no longer dangerous, then the miners said they would go back to work. The whole thing was a trick. They had no intention at all of doing another survey. All they were going to do was to start mining on their own.

"The miners found this out too late. Someone had seen the owners going in with mining tools and reported it. There was a terrific panic in the village and all the miners came rushing up the valley to the mine. They must have looked a fierce army, armed with mining picks and staves. Before they could reach the mine, a large explosion shook the ground.

"The owners were killed. The mark of a claw was left, as usual, on the rock above the bodies. The old mine and its Keepers seemed well able to preserve the village."

Peter interrupted. "You mean you think the mine will try and stop people working it again?"

"Aye, it will. I don't know how, but it will. If it was ever worked again it would mean death to the village. The villagers don't know why, but they do know it will mean death. They think it's haunted but that's not important. The real secret died with the generation of workers. My grandad told my old man and he passed it on to me. He reckoned it would be in the interests of the village for someone to stop it being worked if it was ever found."

"But surely," said Peter, puzzled, "all you have to do is to tell anyone who started to mine it all about the water."

"Yer mean well, lad, but it's not as simple as that. Do you think anyone would believe an old fool like me, living on his own? Once they got a sight of that lead, they'd investigate and the whole lot would come down. The block was built to last as long as it wasn't touched, but remove some of them stones and the whole lot will come down with the pressure of the water. Probably all that's holding the main reservoir now is the stone barrier. There's no need to look worried, lad; the stone is quite a few feet thick and made by experts to last for ever. You may not know this, but just there the passage is pretty close to the hillside. If the mine hadn't been closed, they'd have made another entrance there to save carrying everything back so far. If the water got out, it could break through there and rush down the valley."

"Well, *we'll* tell people about the water," said Tim.

"Aye, yer mean well, lad. But they'd not believe you any more than they'd believe me. They'd ask you how you knew, and then they'd say they would take care just to keep you happy. But would they be careful? They'd laugh behind your back and think it was just a story you'd made up."

Peter could see himself pleading with a company not to mine any further and just being told to run along and play. The more he thought about it, the more worked up he got and he burst out, "What on earth can we do, then?"

Mad Sam smiled. "The mine's well able to look after itself. I don't know how it will do it this time, but I know it will. You can be sure it knows some-one's broken in. They did put a notice up but I expect it's gone by now.

"I've finished my tale so you can run along and fetch a doctor." He started to cough again. "I don't expect he'll be able to do much good. I trust the two of you never to tell the secret of the mine. You now have the responsibility of the lives of the whole village in your hands. It's for you to use or misuse that responsibility. Don't go near the mine again. It might kill you now you know its secret. It's not a friendly mine even though it's guarding the village."

Mad Sam closed his eyes and sighed. "Now, be off," he faltered.

Peter had been tidying up the bed while the old

man was finishing, and when Mad Sam stopped they hurried from the house.

"He looked pretty ill," panted Peter as they ran.

"Mmm. I shouldn't think there's much hope for him. Good thing he told us about all that water, because if he'd died we might easily have told people where the mine is."

The doctor was called and the old man taken away to hospital. Soon after dinner the vicar told the boys that he had died. This came as a shock to Peter and Tim.

Peter turned to Mr. Parkinson. "I don't really understand." He looked worried. "About Mad Sam dying, I mean. Both Tim and I prayed that he would recover. Why didn't he?"

Mr. Parkinson sat down. "That sort of thing worries most people. We can't tell God what to do, but that doesn't mean we shouldn't ask for these things. We've got to learn to accept His way, though."

"I suppose everyone has to die sometime," reflected Tim. "To a Christian, of course, it's something to look forward to. Didn't St. Paul say something about that?"

Peter frowned. "Didn't he say he would rather die and be with Jesus, but he had work to do for Jesus while he was here?"

Mr. Parkinson nodded. "The thought that we are going to die, or that Jesus may come back in our lifetime, should keep us on our toes as Christians. Some people have a long life and still never

want to turn from their own ways and let God live
in their lives."

"There's no point in leaving it to the last
moment," said Tim. "At least, I'm glad I became
a Christian when I did."

Mrs. Parkinson could see that they were upset
and that a rest to help forget about it would be just
the thing. So she suggested that they drove to
Derby for a shopping expedition.

Although they wanted to get back to the mine
and make a plan of it, the boys realised that it
would probably be better if they were to get away
from things for a bit, so they decided to go. Apart
from the odds and ends that one usually buys when
visiting a large city, they bought nothing special.
But Mrs. Parkinson, judging by their appetites at
tea, realised that the afternoon had done them
good. Instead of going straight home they drove
round the Derbyshire countryside for a bit, enjoy-
ing the views. Their minds were also taken off
things during the evening for they helped in some
church activities.

The Timpitters tumbled into bed having almost
forgotten about Mad Sam and his secret of the
mine. Indeed, their minds had been taken off
things so much that they had forgotten completely
about his warning that they should never enter the
mine again.

K

Chapter 14

A RACE AGAINST TIME

Once again Peter and Tim stood by the entrance
to the mine. This time they had brought no rucksack with them and had worn their caving clothing
to the mine. They had left their ladders and ropes
behind as they were only going to do a rough survey and make a map. The only equipment they
carried, apart from spare carbide for the lamps,
was their camera and their short lengths of nylon
waist ropes. Peter had a notebook and pencil.

The survey was to be just a rough plan drawn to
measurements from pacing, and, in the case of pacing being impossible, approximations. They had a
pocket compass to help them get the general direc-
tion of the passages. It took them some time to
reach the chamber with the water in it, where they
had tried to wade when they first found it. This
time, to their surprise, the water was considerably
lower and they could see that the deep part where
Tim had disappeared under water was the mouth
of a shaft. The rails ran right to the edge of it, and
the boys assumed that the miners had pushed all
the trucks from the lower series down in their at-
tempt to stop the mine being worked. The shaft
had then probably filled with water in the course
of years and the level altered from time to time as

it soaked away. The storm that had blown up a few days before had probably filled it temporarily. The passage hardly went any way beyond the shaft, and they were glad they had not gone to the trouble of getting a raft or boat.

They climbed the iron ladder and explored the side passage in the very large chamber. This was a natural passage, running fairly steeply uphill. It got too narrow after a few yards and they had to admit defeat and return. Peter entered this on the plan and then looked up at Tim.

"You know, we'll have to give this chamber a name. We can't just draw it as a nameless cavern on the plan. Any suggestions?"

Tim looked for inspiration by searching the gloom with his lamp.

"How about Monster Cavern?" he said after a bit.

"Where's the monster?"

"There isn't a monster, ass. I was referring to the size."

"Oh well, that's fine," laughed Peter. "I'll put it down."

He wrote it on the rather muddy plan and then said, "I think we could call the way on 'Suicide Passage' after our narrow escape . . . when the mine tried to kill us."

"I say, you don't think . . . ?"

"What? That the mine would really try to kill us, as Mad Sam said? Of course not; that was a lot of rot. I believe what he said about the water, though, and we can check up on that when we get to the wall and see the warning—or what's left of it. He could never have been down here so if there are any remains of the writing he must have been telling the truth. Come on."

They paced out the passage, passed the chamber where their truck had fallen down the shaft and reached the Dragon's Claw. There they saw the warning painted on the wall, which they had missed the last time. Most of it had been washed away by water and time. Moisture running down the wall had left a deposit over the remaining parts, but they could make out the word 'WATER' and they knew the old man had been correct.

Tim shuddered at the thought of all the water that lay behind that rock.

"Let's get back," he said, his voice rather shaky although he tried to control it. "I tell you, I feel rather nervous about this place . . . Ssssh, what's that?"

"What's what?"

"I thought I heard a rumbling sound, but it was probably imagination. It would be pretty horrible if there was a roof fall, wouldn't it? Let's go!"

"Okay, I suppose you're right. We've just about surveyed the lot and photographed all there is to photograph, so we'll make our way back."

Tim took one last look around. "Just fancy, there's enough water behind there to flood a village."

Peter frowned. "It's lucky these underground reservoirs are rare. It's unfortunate that there happens to be one under the moor but there's not much we can do about it except keep it secret. You can see this block is built to last. The village wouldn't be in danger unless it was pulled down. See how all the stones are in a sort of wedge so the water pressure would only bind them closer together? I wouldn't like to pull a stone out! It's funny we should have thought it was a fall the first time we saw it. I suppose it was because of all this loose stone lying about."

Peter lingered on the way out, looking at the sights for what was probably to be the last time. "Too bad," he thought, "that we'll have to close the mine for good when we go home."

The only consolation was the thought that they were probably preserving the life of the villagers. The thought struck Peter as being quite ridiculous. To think that he and Tim had started out looking for a mine that was shown on a print, to find a mine with such a tremendous secret. What an adventure! Not with smugglers or any other people but with a mystery mine which endangered a whole village. The mystery had indeed turned out to be a grim secret.

Peter smiled as they passed the beam that had nearly beheaded him. The lamp on his helmet would always bear the mark of that brief encounter. But the wooden beam was also marked. Tim pointed this out to Peter.

"You were pretty lucky not to bring the whole thing down, Peter. One good shake would dislodge the lot. We might have been cut off for good."

"Do you think so? How about it, then? How

about collapsing it now? That at least would dis-
courage anyone from going further even if they
did get as far as this."

This was not one of Peter's most brilliant suggestions but at the time it seemed quite good. Anyway, Tim agreed to it and they set about putting
the plan into action. Peter had brought some tough
string to help with the measurements and with this
they resolved to pull one of the main timbers away.
First they had to loosen the chosen one sufficiently.

"If you hold on here, Tim, I'll pull gently at
this end."

At first nothing happened and then it swung
loose with alarming speed. If Tim had not had
tight hold of the slippery wood, the whole lot
would have come crashing down round them,
bringing many tons of rock.

After some tense moments the trap was sprung
and, taking care to pay the string out gently, the
boys retreated along the passage.

When they reached the limit of the string they
paused and took a big breath. They had hardly
spoken. Peter looked up at the roof and moved
his head so that the light flashed over it
thoroughly.

"This part's sound enough," he remarked. "I
think we should be okay. Be ready, just in case."

"How?"

"Dunno. Ready? Here goes!"

The beam came away very easily. Too easily,
Peter thought afterwards, when he considered
how he had stood by it when fixing the string.

There was no steady creaking. The whole lot came down in one go. One moment there was silence and the next a good section of the passage was down.

But that was not the end of it. The sound could be heard reverberating along the passages, bringing down miniature falls in places. Then they heard something through the walls. Another loud crash, only this time quite muffled. Slowly Peter pulled their plan from his pocket, and for the first time he realised how close they were to the lower level they had first entered.

Tim, looking over his shoulder, had also seen this, and the two decided they must get out as quickly as possible. They ran, slithered and slipped, but the danger seemed to be past. With relief they slowed to a more normal pace.

They passed the water again and, when they came to the place they had called the Cross Roads where the four passages suddenly converged, Peter stopped suddenly.

"Hey, did you feel anything funny? I thought the ground shook. *It did!* I felt it again. Let's get out of here quickly."

They ran but, when they got to the bridge, to their horror it was missing. As they stood wondering what they should do, from fairly close at hand came a resounding crash followed by another.

"Whew!" cried Peter. "The whole place is coming in. That crash seemed to come from the entrance. Quick! Jump!"

Tim backed a bit and launched himself into space. Peter followed him. He saw the black pit flash underneath and then he landed on the slippery bank opposite.

Having collected everything up, they ran as fast as they could in the narrow passage, but when they got to the entrance it had collapsed completely. They stared at it numbly. Surely it was not possible. Peter was unable to believe it. It was like a dream and he would wake up in a minute and laugh at his fear. But the water he was standing in was real, and so were the black walls, so the roof fall must be real as well. If, and it seemed highly probable, the fall went the whole way back to the entrance, then there was twenty feet of rock separating them from the outside world.

After staring at the rock for what seemed an age, an alternative to staying and starving or getting crushed by further falls dawned on Peter. Admittedly it was a slim chance but it was a possibility.

"We've had it here," he said to Tim. "We'll have to go along the old workings, if they still exist, and try to climb that old shaft. I don't fancy it but it's our only chance. Do hurry! The mine may not have finished collapsing yet."

Although he thought the chances of escape were remote, he kept his views from Tim. If each knew that the other had despaired, their position would be hopeless. While there was hope there was life—perhaps. They rushed and pushed their way along the narrow, twisting passages, knocking themselves badly on the narrow, jagged walls but hardly noticing it. They had only one thought in mind, and

that was to reach daylight as soon as possible. The
first shaft they climbed without difficulty.

They charged past the tomb where the miners,
or Keepers as Mad Sam had called them, who had
died in the Plague were buried, and from there
into the very old workings where going was slow
as the passage was unstable. One good jolt on a
wooden beam might bring the whole lot down.
They realised this only too well. Never had a mile
seemed so long, but even in their fright Peter could
still put first things first. "We must pause and pray,
Tim. Pray!"

Both realised how foolishly they had acted and
now, as they prayed, they not only asked God, their
Heavenly Father, to protect them and to help
them to get out of their present dangerous position, but also that He would forgive their stupidity
and enable them to use more common-sense in
future.

After they had prayed, Tim remarked, "We
should have learnt our lesson now. After all, God
has given us common-sense so that we may put it
to good use."

But there was no time for further delay, and
they set off again and came to a slightly wider
and straighter bit where they were able to run.
Their lamps hissed in the wind and Peter realised
that it was not only a race against time as far as
danger from the mine was concerned but also as
far as the life of their lamps was concerned. They
had refilled them once but the time for refilling
must be drawing near again. Even as he thought

this his lamp suddenly dimmed. He turned on more water but nothing happened. Was the end, he wondered, drawing near?

The way they completed that mile was incredible. Sometimes crawling, sometimes running, and often pausing at slight sounds to listen if the mine was falling in, they finally reached the pile of rock that marked the foot of the shaft. They looked upwards and realised it was not going to be such an easy climb after all. It had certainly seemed quite possible when it was unlikely they would ever have to climb it, but now they really had to do it their nerve started to fail. However, urged on by necessity, they quickly decided who should climb first and the lot fell to Tim. He turned and gave Peter a faint smile. Peter was in a strange situation. He wanted Tim to get out safely and yet he wanted him to stay. The thought of being left alone was frightening. For a moment they stood, asking Jesus to give them strength. Then Tim, urged on by a further crash in the mine, suddenly darted for the shaft and started climbing.

Tim was fully aware that the mine was still collapsing, and he climbed furiously. Peter had given him a leg up to start and soon he was going quite quickly. The shaft might even have been built for climbing, for with his back sliding up one wall there were plenty of foot-holds opposite. In spite of the speed at which he was climbing, he felt completely worn out by the time he had done fifty feet, and then he was only a quarter of the way up. The perspiration was standing out on his forehead, partly because of the exertion and partly because of his fear. He paused to rest and look down. There was a faint glow cast by Peter's lamp.

Peter, who had heard the rattle of stones stop, called up to ask if anything was wrong. The faint hope that Tim had reached the top was shattered when Tim shouted back that he had not got far. It was not very pleasant being left alone at the bottom, waiting for his friend to make one false move and come hurtling down. Tim shouted that he was starting off again, and Peter went through the agony of suspense once more. All he could do was to put his trust in God's help. After a few minutes Tim called down once again.

"I can't hear," Peter called back.

Tim's voice came back faintly. "Come up."

Peter acknowledged the call and made his way to the shaft. He had been standing some distance away from it, for safety. Without anyone to help, the beginning bit was quite tricky, but he soon got the hang of it and found it quite easy going as Tim had done. As soon as he was within easy calling distance of Tim, he asked him if he was out.

Tim said he wasn't but there was a cavity where he was sheltering. Peter joined him and lay panting and shaking on the uneven floor.

Tim, who had rested, got up to resume his climb.

"I shouldn't think we're more than half-way up," he said. "It's going to be tougher now we're getting to the looser stone. I don't know how we're going to get past all that wood at the top. Keep well in, won't you, while I'm climbing."

As Tim finished speaking, a deep boom ran through the mine and even the shaft vibrated.

"Peter!" said Tim, panicking, "It shook; the shaft shook!"

He drew back as a large stone, dislodged by the vibration, came hurtling down the shaft to splinter into smithereens at the bottom.

Peter sounded calm although he felt far from it.

"I should think the whole mine has more or less collapsed now. I'll go first, if you like," he offered.

"No, I'd rather go first and get it over, if you don't mind."

Tim disappeared from view with his kicking legs searching for a foot-hold. Peter heaved a big sigh and waited for his turn. They had only themselves to blame for the mine collapsing. Mad Sam had believed in superstition, but Peter trusted in God. All he *could* do now was to trust God.

Occasionally a large stone whistled by, making Peter jump. Tim shouted something he could not hear. One loud shout and something started to fall in the shaft. Peter heard it bouncing from side to side as it fell. It flashed by and landed at the bottom with a thud. It was no rock. It had been something soft.

"In which case," reasoned Peter with a peculiar calmness, "it must have been Tim."

He had come to this conclusion without its full significance sinking in. Then a sort of numbness seized his mind, and what seemed like lightning tore across his brain, almost tearing him in half.

Tim fallen? It couldn't be true—*must* not be true. "Please, Lord, don't let it be Tim."

He called out feebly. The only answer he got was a few stones rattling down the shaft. Stones rattling down the shaft? Then surely . . . no, it couldn't be.

"Tim!" he called really loudly, *"Tim!"*

From somewhere, an answering shout came, but he could not tell if it came from above or below.

"Well," he reasoned, "it must be from above because no one could fall nearly two hundred feet and live. In which case he's still okay. Thank you, Lord, thank you!"

Peter soon got the all clear from Tim and he started to climb. The limestone was crumbling and his lamp was burning unsteadily. When he got nearly to the top he almost slipped when a piece of earth gave way. He lay braced across the shaft, unable to move. His muscles had set and however hard he tried to move he just couldn't.

Tim, ready to help as usual, lowered his short rope, which Peter with some difficulty managed to clip onto the one round his waist. Then Tim helped him out.

"I say," said Tim quite cheerfully, "I hope that dead sheep missed you. I found it on a ledge and had to kick it down, but I did shout to warn you. And pooh, didn't it stink!"

Peter looked at his friend and started to laugh. After every adventure their friendship seemed to be made stronger. There was still much they were finding out about each other—and about God, too.

Getting up, Peter brushed the grass off hi
boiler-suit.

"Oh well, Tim," he said, "we can't sit here al
day. Let's go and get the remains of the entranc
covered properly. Oh yes, tomorrow I suppose we
ought to have a look at that cave of yours at Eyam
—just to make sure you're really satisfied with
this holiday! *Come on!*"